Fig. 2.

Craniometer.

THEORIES OF IDEATION

THEORIES OF

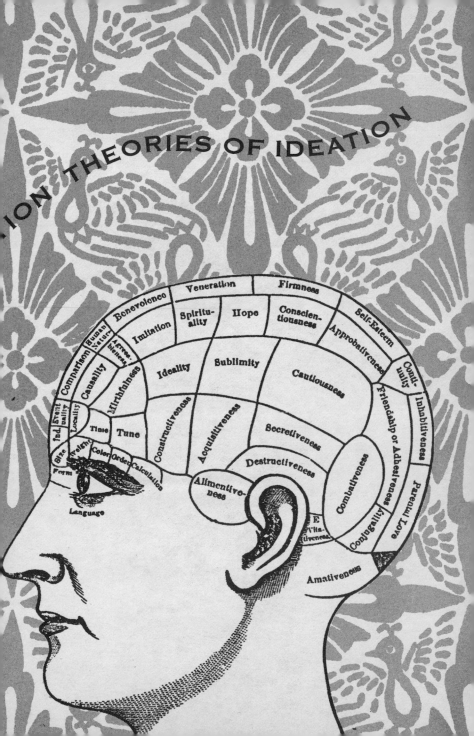

THEORIES OF IDEATION

BONE DRY

KATHLEEN KARR

BONE DRY

HYPERION PAPERBACKS FOR CHILDREN

NEW YORK

Text copyright © 2002 by Kathleen Karr

First Hyperion Paperback Edition, 2003
1 3 5 7 9 10 8 6 4 2

Printed in the United States of America

Map art by Alfred Giuliani

Library of Congress Cataloging-in-Publication Data on file.
ISBN 0-7868-1594-9 (pbk.)

Visit www.hyperionchildrensbooks.com

For Donna Bray

Both the man of science and the man of action
live always at the edge of mystery. . . .

—*J. Robert Oppenheimer*

ROUTE OF
DR. ASA B. CORNWALL
AND MATTHEW MORRISSEY
THROUGH NORTHERN AFRICA

TRIPOLI

GADAMES

TIMBUKTU

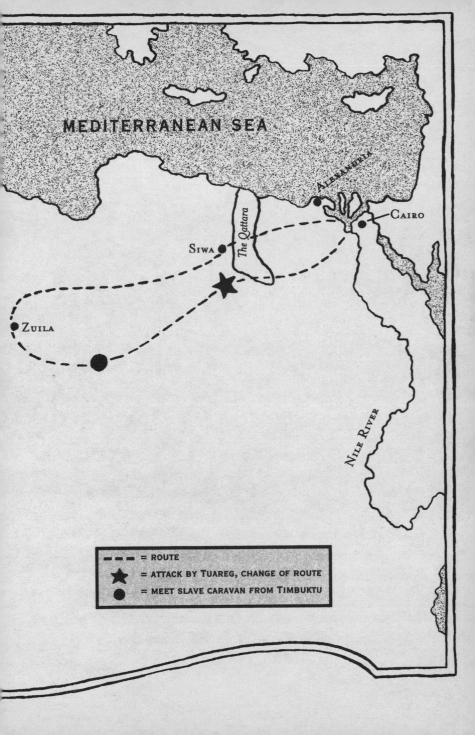

MEDITERRANEAN SEA

ALEXANDRIA

CAIRO

SIWA

The Qattara

ZUILA

NILE RIVER

- - - = ROUTE
★ = ATTACK BY TUAREG, CHANGE OF ROUTE
● = MEET SLAVE CARAVAN FROM TIMBUKTU

THERE WERE NO MAPS. IT WAS UNCHARTED TERRITORY. Matthew Morrissey sat astride his camel, willing his body to ease into the stumbling gait that was like nothing so much as riding an earthquake. Not that he'd ever experienced an earthquake, but at this point in his fourteen years he firmly believed it to be one of the few things he had not yet experienced. That, too, might come. The feeling was inescapable.

Ahead of him their Arab guide, Hussein, blazed the trail. Beside him his dog, Gin, loped through the sand. Behind, Asa B. Cornwall, in a state of perpetual panic, clung to his own camel. Bringing up the rear of the caravan were a dozen camel drivers and guards. All had impressive swords slung from their shoulders and myriad daggers hidden beneath their robes. Surrounding them was nothing and everything: the Great Sahara.

Another fine mess he'd gotten himself into. Where had this one begun? On the ragged cliffs of St. Helena, where he and Dr. Cornwall had tried for Napoleon's skull, or much earlier, back in a New York cemetery, where he'd had his first glimpse of the body snatcher? Matthew mulled over his strange fate, trying to probe its deepest roots.

So enmeshed was he in memories that he never noticed the vast sand dune their small caravan was approaching, never noticed something curiously marring its pure silhouette: the telltale glint of hot sun reflected from burnished steel. . . .

Alexander the Great

CHAPTER ONE

Perhaps it had begun in Paris, on the boulevard du Crime. Begun with the flaming torches . . .

Higher and higher Matthew tossed the torches into a crisp blue spring sky. Balanced confidently on the shoulders of the acrobat beneath him, he reveled in the gestures that had come so easily to him in these past few months under the training of his new friends. He felt again the emotion that had made the skill irresistible to him from the start. Juggling was a kind of resurrection. It was a

1

game that freed his mind, taking him far above
the depths of the graves in which he'd spent too
much time. And juggling with *fire* felt like making
an offering to the sky and heaven above it. It was
a little moment of pardon asked—and forgiveness
granted—for the profession he practiced with Dr.
Cornwall.

A carriage paused among the throng before
him, its matched pair of horses tossing their fine
heads. Matthew flung a last round into the fir-
mament, then caught the torches one by one. He
blew out the first, then another. But the third
flaming torch was his finale. Instead of extin-
guishing it, he drew the flames into his mouth,
then spewed them forth in a stream of fire that
almost reached the crested door of the carriage.
Still balanced on the strong body below him,
Matthew swept into a bow. The carriage window
came down. There was the brief glimpse of a
lightly veiled face: the countess who came often
to admire his new skill. She tossed up a coin.
Matthew caught it and bounded to earth with
another bow. The carriage moved on.

"It's gold!" He flipped it to his partner, Étienne.

"*Merci*, Matthieu. But your share?"

"It's all yours today, *mon ami*. A present for
teaching me your art." He hesitated, unwilling to
admit even to himself that he'd soon have to leave

this place he'd come to love. He glanced down the grand avenue lined with panoramas, theaters of melodrama and pantomime, food stalls, puppet shows, acrobats, and musicians—all lustily plying their trades to the passing crowds. The bright sun added another level of gaiety to the scene, making it even harder for him. This had been his true home during the months Dr. Cornwall had been closeted in their hotel suite, finishing his phrenological *magnum opus*. Matthew swallowed hard. "I have to go away for a while."

"Matthieu—" His friend's face turned crest-fallen. "Do you go very far away?"

To *Siwa*, wherever that was. Dr. Cornwall had made the announcement this morning. Just the one word. To Siwa, in search of Alexander the Great.

Matthew clapped Étienne's shoulder. "Very far, I fear."

"You'll return?"

"God willing, Étienne. But now I must make the rest of my farewells. *Au revoir.*"

Matthew turned away quickly. Partings were painful. Nearby, his dog barked once, reminding him how patiently Gin had been waiting through the entire performance. He deserved a reward. Matthew grabbed for Gin's leash and moved toward the nearest stall.

"*Ça va*, Monsieur Lacenaire?"

"*Ça va*, Matthieu." Jacques Lacenaire readjusted his beret and leaned over the counter of his booth to point below at the newly painted image of a fat, laughing pig.

"Ah," said Matthew admiringly. "*Quel beau cochon!*"

The proud proprietor beamed. "*Un saucisson pour Jeen?*"

"*Mais, oui.*"

Matthew passed a coin to Lacenaire, and presently Gin was wolfing down a very large sausage. Gin ate his way along another length of the boulevard, until the two stood before the Théâtre du Vaudeville, where the magician Robert-Houdin sometimes exhibited his skills.

Matthew found Robert-Houdin backstage, pulling bouquet after bouquet of brilliantly colored artificial flowers from the sleeves of his frock coat.

"*Bonjour, monsieur.*"

"*Voilà, est-ce vous, Matthieu?* Just in time. I was about to practice *The Aerial Suspension.*"

"I haven't time to float in midair today, *monsieur.* I'm on an errand for my master."

The magician focused on Matthew, another bouquet suspended halfway out his cuff. "So. His book is complete at last and he returns to the world?"

Matthew nodded. "*Dr. ABC's ABCs of Phrenology: From the Skull Out.* It goes to press tomorrow, and soon we'll be off to faraway places again."

"*Quel dommage.* You showed promise, young man."

"*Merci, monsieur.* It's been an honor to learn from you. You'll have your own theater soon, I'm sure. People will be clamoring to buy tickets to see the great Robert-Houdin, just as they do now for Deburau the mime."

The magician raised an elegant eyebrow. "*Peut-être.* When I've perfected my *Fantastic Orange Tree*—"

"You will, *monsieur.*"

Robert-Houdin nodded acceptance of the inevitable. "Give your master my regards. I look forward to reading his great work."

"I shall. *Adieu.*"

Regretfully, Matthew hauled Gin from the avenue of so many pleasures and temptations. They wandered through narrow, twisting streets, arriving finally before the bookshop where he'd spent his other free hours since he and Dr. Cornwall had returned on the flotilla bearing Napoleon's body in state. It was a fascinating hole-in-the-wall, crammed from floor to ceiling with the most exotic books in the strangest languages.

"*Librairie du Monde.*" Matthew read the sign aloud

with satisfaction. Even its name was evocative. "Come along, Gin. It's time to pay our respects to Monsieur Baltone."

The inside of the shop was as dark and cavelike as ever. Its elderly proprietor sat bent over one of his books, mumbling words aloud as his finger ran down a page. Matthew cleared his throat.

"*Qui est-ce?*" The gray head jerked up. "Matthieu. What can we share this afternoon?"

"Siwa, *monsieur?*"

"Ah, the desert. The Sahara."

"So there aren't any maps. Or any books, for that matter." Asa B. Cornwall was testy. "That means we begin with a *tabula rasa*. That's Latin for 'empty slate'—"

"I know, sir. I've been studying Latin in your absence."

"My absence?" Cornwall tugged at his rumpled velvet jacket. "Where've I been, I'd like to know? Right here! Under your nose since January!"

Oatmeal, Matthew said to himself. Time to get Dr. Cornwall back on a diet of oatmeal. Months of rich French sauces weren't helping matters any. Aloud, he continued, "But it seems I should have been studying Arabic the whole time

6

instead. That's what Monsieur Baltone recommended. Even found a primer for me—"

"What about Berber?" snapped Cornwall. "Or the other dialects of the Bedouins? Did he find you primers for them, too?"

"It didn't come up—"

"Of course not. And a dictionary of the Saharan tribal languages probably doesn't exist anyway. That's how much your fine Mr. Baltone knows about Northern Africa!"

"He did have a few things to say about the recent French occupation of Algeria—"

"Bah. We're not going to Algeria. And the rest of the upper African continent is blank. Blank, I tell you! We'll have to begin in Cairo, and our French should be useful enough there. Ah, Alexander the Great!" He patted at his wisps of hair and calmed himself with thoughts of the challenge before them.

"After Napoleon, Alexander was the other supreme military genius of recorded history. He should be worth a complete volume in my phrenological works all by himself!" Cornwall chuckled, then became serious. "We need to pick up his trail where Alexander himself began, in a manner of speaking. On the sands of the great desert of Egypt—"

"But surely he's not buried in the desert, sir," Matthew interrupted.

"Of course not! Siwa is an oasis, hidden deep in the dust of time. It's the site of the oracle of the Temple of Amun, where Alexander went in 331 B.C. to confirm his divinity before setting forth on his conquests. It will inspire us, too!"

"Wouldn't it be easier just to head for the place where he died?"

"Babylon? But he's not buried there, either. We're off on a quest of *understanding*, lad. When we finally meet his skull—presumably in Alexandria, where a great mausoleum was erected in his honor—"

"So it's as straightforward as that?" Matthew asked. "We could just take a boat to Egypt, walk up to his mausoleum, and—"

"Of course it's not as straightforward as that," barked the doctor. "Nothing's that easy!" Cornwall wandered to the nearest window to stare out into the Parisian night. "Alexander's mausoleum disappeared centuries ago. It's going to require some creative research to relocate it. But when we do"—Cornwall spun around to focus on Matthew—"when we do, I want to be able to read more than the bumps on his skull. I want the *subtleties*, too." Cornwall began pacing around their sitting room. "First thing in the morning, do some research on camels."

"Camels?" Matthew asked.

"Yes, camels. And begin buying up all the quinine to be found in the local apothecaries."

"Quinine?"

"Malaria, lad. Africa is vicious with it. As for me, the moment I've finished with my publisher, I'll head for the Louvre and its Egyptology collections. Must see what the papyrus scrolls have to say about possible antidotes for scorpion bites—"

"Scorpion bites!" Matthew gulped.

"Stop parroting me, boy. We're going where no American—or European, for that matter—has gone before. At least for the last few thousand years. I like to be prepared."

"Yes, sir." Matthew glanced down at Gin. "What about him, Doctor? Can he come with us?"

"Never heard of a dog getting malaria, have you?"

Matthew grinned. "No sir, I haven't."

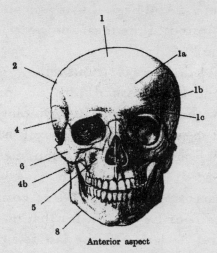

Anterior aspect

CHAPTER TWO

"WE'RE LEAVING HENRY BEDLOW?"

Matthew had begun packing, but found himself distracted by the row of skulls marching across their sitting room's mantelpiece: Henry Bedlow, Aaron Burr, Nicholas Mordecai, Jean-Jacques Rousseau. It was a rogues' gallery of his recent past, more chilling than all the museums of waxworks on the boulevard du Crime.

"We've got to travel light this time, lad."

"But Henry Bedlow? He's always been our

touchstone, always given us our motivation for greater things—"

"And so he still shall," allowed Cornwall. "But he'll do it from a continent's distance, in storage with the rest of our collection."

Matthew patted Henry's varnished cranium for old times' sake. He was rewarded with the usual gaping, ironic smile. "It doesn't seem right. . . . Does that mean you're also leaving your phrenological instruments behind?"

"Don't be absurd!" The doctor was currently stuffing a freshly printed copy of his *magnum opus* into his ratty old leather satchel. "I'd feel naked without them when we come head-to-head with Alexander. Pack the calipers and craniometer," he ordered, "but leave the phrenological bust and charts. Push comes to shove, the tools could prove useful beforetimes, too. And they don't take up much room."

"True," Matthew agreed. He opened an empty trunk and began carefully shrouding Bedlow for his interim entombment.

They departed Paris for the southern port of Toulon, carrying only the clothes on their backs, two personal satchels, and an emergency medical bag filled with quinine and other nostrums that

11

the doctor had decreed necessary for their well-being in unknown territories. They also carried—on their persons—the final gold coins from their war chest, along with a letter of credit to a financial establishment in Cairo.

Through the coach window Matthew cast a last long glance at Paris disappearing behind them. Then he laid a hand atop Gin's head for his own reassurance. "What happens if we run out of money, sir? Bribing all those French bureaucrats for passage to St. Helena took a heavy toll on our resources."

"Eh?" Cornwall's head popped up from his *magnum opus*, which he was rereading for the umpteenth time. Its hand-cut pages were already beginning to show wear. "Money? One of my new rules, Matthew, is never to worry about money. We have sufficient for the needs of our current expedition."

"After that?" Matthew pressed. "What then?"

"Providence will provide, lad. Always has." Dr. ABC returned his nose to his book, mumbling, "Quite a cogent point I make here regarding Napoleon's sanguine physiology. . . ."

The worries were left to Matthew, as usual.

Matthew's anxieties evaporated long before they

reached Toulon. Worse came to worst, he decided, he could always keep the doctor and Gin fed with his recently acquired juggling skills. There were other uses for these skills, too, he soon learned. A few hours out of port he stood in the bow of the ship inspecting the Mediterranean Sea spread out before him as he absently kept three oranges suspended in the air.

"How wonderful!"

Matthew automatically caught the falling spheres as he spun. It was a girl. No, a young lady. A very pretty young lady. He gave a bow worthy of the countess of the boulevard du Crime. *"Mademoiselle—"*

"Please don't stop. It's the nicest thing I've seen all day."

"Not the sea?" The oranges sprang to life again. The sea was as deeply blue as the young lady's eyes, Matthew noted.

Those eyes veered from the view. "After making this voyage so many times, the sea no longer impresses me."

"Why would you make such a long voyage so many times?" Matthew feigned a slight indifference as his hands continued their gravity-defying work.

It all came out, then. Her father was Egyptian, her mother French. Her family shared each year between two homelands, but she felt secure in neither. What also came out was her name.

"Nathalie."

Matthew pocketed the oranges to run fingers through his windswept hair. It was as black and curly as hers. "Matthew. Matthew Morrissey. Perhaps we can be some company to each other on this particular voyage."

"Nathalie!"

A hunted look entered her eyes. "It's Papa. I must go."

As she disappeared, Matthew thoughtfully set his oranges spinning again.

Matthew and Dr. Cornwall shared dinner in the salon that evening with Nathalie and her father. Her mother did not make an appearance then, or during the entire voyage. Abdullah Abed chose not to remark upon her absence. He was a modern Arab businessman, dark and sleek, clean-shaven and richly attired—from his tailored black tailcoat to his silk waistcoat with pearl buttons, right up to the gold-embroidered fez upon his head. He and the doctor began an animated conversation about Alexander's role in the history of Egypt that continued throughout the meal. But try as he might, Matthew could not accomplish the same with Abdullah Abed's daughter. She sat across from him, her eyes modestly focused on her plates and utensils through the entire course of the meal. It was not till afterward, when Matthew stood alone under moonlight and sails, that he discovered the reasons.

She materialized out of the shadows, all mystery.

"Nathalie!"

"Papa may appear modern"—she clung to the railing, her grasp tense and tight—"but he prefers to treat Maman and me as his private possessions, keeping us cut off from the dangers of the world."

Matthew was too enchanted to pursue her complaint. It was enough that she was here beside him.

From that moment the two were inseparable during discrete periods of the journey. Their hours together were regulated by her father's quirks. He slept late; napped away most of the afternoon; retired early to work on business affairs. Matthew and Nathalie shared these secure interludes. He showed her the Arab primer he was struggling with, and she tutored him. She was a patient teacher, and he a quick student. The weeks of the voyage flew past.

Asa B. Cornwall's friendship with Abdullah

Abed proved fruitful as well. When their ship docked in Alexandria at last, it was Abed who smoothed their way; Abed who made room on his private *felucca* for the much shorter voyage up the Nile to Cairo. And it was Abed who opened his palatial home to Dr. Cornwall, Matthew, and Gin while preparations were made for their expedition to Siwa. Finally, it was Abdullah Abed who secured for them the services of a general factotum and guide into the desert. That is how they came to be under the protection of Hussein.

"Lie down, son of an asp!"

Hussein solidly thwacked the rear end of a camel. Its head and long neck lunged for Hussein's body, but its teeth caught nothing but the hem of the man's robe. Groaning with frustration, the camel collapsed joint by joint onto the dirt of the stable courtyard.

"You." Hussein pointed at Matthew. "Approach and mount. But be vigilant. Ali is a scoundrel. He cares for nothing but the taste of human flesh."

That was not a ringing recommendation. Matthew edged up to the beast warily and lifted a leg to straddle the rug-covered wooden saddle atop Ali's hump.

"Stop!"

He jumped back. "What did I do wrong, sir?"

"I am not some fine infidel, *sir*," growled the wiry bantam cock of a man. He was shorter than Matthew, but when he puffed out his chest, he overcame the difference. "I am *Hussein*, follower of Allah, master of camels and men!"

"Absolutely, sir. I mean, Hussein—"

"You must remove your shoes and stockings. A proper Arab guides the camel with his toes."

"Barefoot?"

"You wish to go into the Western Desert? You wish to survive more than a few days in this desert?"

"Yes," breathed Matthew.

"Then you will learn our ways." Hussein waved toward a pile of robes lying nearby. "You will dress as an Arab, wearing the *gallibiya* on your body, wrapping your head as I do. You will go barefoot. If not, the desert raiders will see you and your master as the Christian pigs you are. And then—"

"And then *what*?" Matthew whispered.

Hussein made a slitting gesture across his throat. "You will reach your Christian paradise sooner than you might wish."

Matthew sank onto the ground next to the camel and made short work of removing his boots. "You might have the right idea after all, Ali," he murmured to the creature. "Certain human flesh cries out for biting."

The camel whickered understanding, and when Matthew climbed upon his back at last, Ali rose without protest. The two were companionably circling the courtyard when Dr. Cornwall appeared. He had come from the arcade that paraded through Abed's walled gardens, linking his fortress of a house to the stables beyond. Gin was at his heels and stopped cold, sniffing the alien smells, while Cornwall squinted through the sun.

"Coming along swimmingly, I see, lad."

"Positively, sir. Now it's your turn for lessons." Matthew chuckled with hidden glee. This should be sport worth watching, he thought.

"Remove my shoes? My good Hussein, these shoes have not been removed in daylight since the cobbler set them upon my feet! . . . Retire my coat for a nightgown? Surely you jest!"

To prove his lack of humor, this time Hussein flourished a dagger to illustrate his point about desert raiders. Then he turned conciliatory.

"For you, *effendi*, I have a pearl of a camel." He beckoned to a stable boy who led forth a second of the animals from the inner stalls. "She is called Fatima, and her nature is as gentle as the flow of her name."

By this time jacketless and hopping painfully from one bare foot to the other to avoid the blistering heat of the earth, Cornwall seemed less than convinced. Fatima lowered herself gracefully and the doctor heaved himself atop her hump. Then she rose.

"Whoa! Wait! Stop!" Asa B. Cornwall clung frantically with every piece of his anatomy till the camel had reached her full height and the doctor dangled six feet above the ground. "No! Matthew! Help!"

Across the courtyard Matthew roared with laughter. He bent to pat Ali's neck. "Are we still going to Siwa, sir? Or—"

His face livid, Cornwall made a supreme effort to master his situation. Legs and arms untangled themselves till he was perched lopsidedly atop his camel. He took a deep breath, then made the fatal error of loosing the death grip of one hand to swipe at his rapidly reddening pate. Fatima chose this moment to move.

"Matth-eeew!"

And Cornwall lay in a pile on the dirt.

"Doctor!" Matthew vaulted over Ali's head and rushed to his side. "Are you hurt? Is anything broken?"

Limb by limb, Cornwall gathered himself together. "Only my pride. Lend me an arm, lad."

Asa B. Cornwall remounted his camel.

Hussein stood back, observing everything. He spoke at last. "*Effendi* truly desires to broach the desert."

"*Effendi* truly does," Cornwall replied with dignity.

"Then it shall be done."

Matthew shook his head and turned back to his own camel. He found Ali resettled in the dust, nose to nose with Gin. He watched his dog fastidiously lick the camel's muzzle, and Ali's huge tongue flick out to return the favor. The heat of the midday sun fell more lightly upon Matthew's shoulders. East could meet West.

Matthew wandered in the gardens under a crescent moon, reveling in the cool night breeze. He paused by the fountain to plunge his fingers into the flowing water.

"Matthieu."

He became a statue, frozen in place. But his voice still worked. "I missed you these past days and hoped you would come. We leave before dawn."

"Papa has had me locked in my room since our return to Cairo. Since he discovered our friendship on the voyage. But I bribed my maid to let me out tonight."

At the satisfied smile in her voice, Matthew's limbs unfroze. He turned. "How could he do that to you, Nathalie?"

"You don't understand the ways of the East yet, Matthieu. In Paris, I am almost free. But here—" She stopped. "At least we are not forced to wear the veil, my mother and I. And Maman also saw to it that I was educated." Her words turned bitter. "Such a magnanimous gesture from my father, when he knows he'll never allow me the liberty of using my education. He almost treats me like one of his—"

"What?" Matthew asked. "Like one of his servants?"

"No. Much worse." Nathalie came close, very close. She reached up to Matthew's face. "This scar. Shaped like tonight's moon. Tell me about this scar. I've wanted to touch it since first we met."

Matthew froze again. "It—it's a very long story, from a time in my life I'd rather forget."

"But it is an honorable scar."

"Yes." He stood taller. "A very honorable scar."

"I knew this. You will be an honorable man . . . if you survive the desert. It is bad enough in winter, but in summer when few wise men go . . ."

Matthew reached for her hand and brought it down to touch his lips. A slight scuffling sound from the edge of the garden made her pull away.

"Be on guard every moment in the desert, Matthieu," she whispered. "There, nothing is as it seems."

Nathalie evaporated into her natural place, the shadows, leaving Matthew to finger the souvenir the body snatcher had left on his cheek.

CHAPTER THREE

Matthew gasped.

The rays of the rising sun struck the dim shapes they'd been riding toward since leaving Cairo in predawn darkness. Gloriously erupting from the flat landscape were the Sphinx and the Great Pyramids of Egypt.

"Doctor! Look!"

"Yes, Matthew. One of the Seven Wonders of the ancient world. These Egyptians really knew how to go out in style!"

The camels had stopped of their own accord. Perhaps they were overwhelmed by the sight as well. Matthew was spellbound, thoughts of beauty, and tremendous age, and history singing in his head.

Cornwall managed to nudge his camel forward next to Matthew's. "It occurs to me, lad, that the mummies of the pharaohs—Cheops, Chephren, the whole lot—might make a very interesting phrenological study once we've dealt with Alexander."

The bubble burst. Matthew toed his camel's neck in frustration, and Ali strode forward. "Hussein!" he shouted ahead. "Where do we meet the rest of our party?"

"Just beyond the Pyramids, *nasrani*. They wait."

Nasrani, Matthew grumbled to himself. That's what Hussein had taken to calling him, and the term was another aggravation. Unlike *effendi*—the title of respect given an educated man—*nasrani* was Arabic for "despised stranger," and was used almost exclusively for Christians. Not that Hussein was aware of Matthew's knowledge. He'd been listening to bits of conversations, keeping his Arabic to himself, thinking it was one of those skills best saved for emergencies. He would swallow the insult, bide his time, and see.

Ali shook his head in protest, distracting Matthew from his grievances. "Sorry, Ali." He loosened his tight grip on the reins that threaded through the camel's nose ring. Ali continued to delicately pick his way through the sands around the Pyramids.

"A rough-looking bunch, I fear," Asa B. Cornwall commented. "Nothing compared to your body snatcher, of course, but still . . ."

The rest of their expedition spread out before them in a long, drunken line facing west and the waiting dunes. Matthew counted twelve men, heavy curved swords slung across their robed shoulders bandolier-style. The faces beneath their white turbans were swarthy, blackened by the sun between wisps of mustaches and beards. These were the camel drivers and guards that Hussein had deemed absolutely necessary for their undertaking to succeed.

"One does not enter the desert without protection, *effendi*," he'd declared during one of their planning sessions.

"But, confound it all," Cornwall complained, "first I'm told no one ever goes into the desert. *Ergo*, it is empty, devoid of human population. Next I'm told any foreigner who does go into the desert is signing his death warrant. It's not logical. If the desert climate is as terrible as the tales told, who in his right mind skulks about in it, waiting like a hungry lion for the odd Christian?"

"Not only Christians, *effendi*."

Hussein refused to say more. Over dinner that evening, Cornwall had broached his complaint to his host, Abdullah Abed.

"But my dear doctor," Abed explained, "there is emptiness, and *emptiness*. Caravan routes have stretched across the Sahara for millennia."

"Then why haven't Europeans heard of them?" Cornwall snapped.

"And why should Europeans—or Americans, for that matter—care about our simple trade routes for transporting salt? Salt is, after all, one of the most basic needs of man." As if to prove his point, Abed spread a pinch of salt over his fish. "None of us can survive without it. No need for you to concern yourself, doctor. Simple precautions are all that Hussein is suggesting. How do the British put it? An ounce of prevention—"

Now Matthew was studying their ounce of prevention. Besides the men there were additional camels: at least twenty riding camels for relief, and several dozen more pack animals, all tethered nose-to-tail and groaning under their loads. Matthew whistled. "All this for just the two of us?"

"What's that, lad?"

"Nothing, doctor. I think Hussein is calling for us."

He was. And soon the caravan was setting off into the Western Desert, the Pyramids and all of civilization disappearing under the scorching blue sky.

"Ooooh."

Cornwall groaned as Matthew helped him off the camel at the end of their first day. "I'll never walk again. I'm too stiff. And my toes! Look— they're blistered from the sun!"

"Here, sir." Matthew handed the doctor a pair of sandals.

"What's this?"

"Apparently sandals are allowed when not riding."

Cornwall glanced suspiciously at their retinue busily unloading camels for the night. "Hah. So they are wearing them. I thought maybe desert Arabs were just naturally born with cast-iron soles."

"Evidently not, sir. They do in fact seem to be human. But most of them also seem to be Bedouins, nomadic people accustomed to the rigors of the desert, rather than Arabs—"

Cornwall bent to struggle into his sandals. "I

haven't the strength for anthropological distinctions at the moment. What must we do next?"

"I think we wait for dinner, sir."

⁓

"*Berr-uuuup.* Ah. *Hamdullah.*"

Massive burps exploded like gunfire from the circle of men surrounding the tiny fire. Matthew surreptitiously wiped his fingers, greasy from the lamb and couscous dinner, on his robe and turned to Cornwall beside him. "First no forks," he whispered. "Everyone just sticking their fingers into the pot. Now this—"

The doctor had enjoyed his meal, vying good-naturedly with the camel drivers for the most succulent morsels of meat. He eased back on his haunches and beamed. "Eructation seems to be one of the social graces around here, Matthew. When in Rome—" and he proceeded to produce a monumental belch.

"*Effendi* enjoyed his food!" murmured the men with approval. Then they stared at Matthew expectantly. It was Hussein who asked the question. "And *nasrani*?"

It had been a long time since Matthew had had flashes of his dead family, but now the memories returned with piercing clarity. The long dinner table in his New York home was strewn with the remains of a huge ham and potatoes, crisp green beans, and thickly sliced bread spread with fresh butter. Amidst the bounty was a much younger Matthew, elbows firmly planted on the table's polished boards, engaged in a spirited burping contest with his little brothers. Raucous laughter filled the air, until his mother systematically cuffed each and every one of her boys.

"Not in my kitchen, at my table, young sirs! I'll teach you all to be gentlemen yet, if I have to beat it into you!"

But the cuffs weren't very hard, and Matthew caught his father grinning into his mug of beer, and his sisters giggling—

Cornwall poked him out of his trance. "They're waiting for an answer, lad."

Matthew felt every eye upon him. His response would have significance. Something churned deep in his belly. He reached for it, coddled it, then brought it forth. The result was the most spectacular of belches, a veritable masterpiece. It took even his breath away as it shook the night sky.

"Bismellah!" It was a very awed "In the name of God," and the utterance came from many lips.

"Hamdullah!" The "Thanks be to God" was equally awed.

Matthew, victorious, glared across the fire

directly into the eyes of Hussein, daring the man to bait him again.

"It is good *nasrani* enjoyed the food," Hussein blandly replied. "It will be the only fresh meat till the first camel dies."

Hussein had bested him. Matthew's stomach cramped with chagrin at Hussein, with loss over his family. He clutched at it until tiny cups of very strong, very sweet tea were passed around. The complete blackness of the desert night overcame him, until not even cup after cup of the hot brew could keep the sudden chill of loneliness from his bones.

The groaning of many camels woke Matthew the next morning. Cornwall was still wrapped in blankets atop his mat, blissfully snoring, so Matthew climbed over the doctor's form to poke his head out the tent flap. A gust of frigid wind sent him back inside for his robe and turban. But even they did little to warm him when he reemerged. He stood hugging his clothing to his body in the half light, wondering how the desert's temperature—which surely had soared well over a hundred degrees only yesterday—could suddenly plummet below freezing with the dawn.

"Tea, *nasrani*?"

Amir, the potbellied expedition cook, handed him the usual thimble-sized cup. Matthew downed it in one gulp. "Thank you." He reached for the gourd being offered. Undoubtedly breakfast. It proved to be a thin millet gruel, bringing back memories of his early oatmeal days with Cornwall. He swallowed gratefully. His shivering slowed, and with the brighter light dawning, he suddenly realized why the camels were making such a god-awful racket. They were on their knees, being loaded for the day: bales of hay, skins of water, the folded tents of the workers. The creatures weren't happy about the situation, and they meant to let the world at large know.

Matthew wandered over to Ali, who was being saddled. Gin was at the camel's side, whining in sympathy. Gin, in fact, had rarely left Ali's side since making his acquaintance. The two animals seemed to share a friendship Matthew had not yet fathomed.

"Good morning, fellows." Matthew bent to ruffle Gin's fur, then pat Ali's nose. "Have you boys had your breakfast gruel?"

"Hussein!" yelled Cornwall around noon of their second day. "When are we stopping for a meal?"

"Tonight, *effendi*."

"Tonight! But I'm hungry now! And by all that's holy, I need to get off this blasted camel to stretch!"

"You may descend to walk at any time you wish, *effendi*."

Cornwall stared at his sunburned toes, then at the scalding sands around him. "But walking would be even hotter!"

"This is true, *effendi*. You show great judgment."

In line directly ahead of Cornwall, Matthew snickered.

"I heard that, Matthew Morrissey!"

"Heard what, sir?"

"Heard—oh, never mind." Cornwall yelled to their guide again. "But what *about* food?"

"Amir will pass some dried meat by and by."

"You mean to say *no one* stops for luncheon?"

"You observed how long it took to prepare the camels this morning, *effendi*?"

"Forever," Cornwall grumbled. "That's how long it took."

Hussein nodded. "Consider, then. The camels have now found their pace. They could walk thus through day, night, and into morning. If we stop them, we must unload them—"

"About two hours to unload, another two to

reload," Matthew contributed from his position between the men.

"*Nasrani* speaks truly. Therefore," Hussein threw back to the doctor, "you must decide. You are the master. For your comfort we will halt. But if you wish to arrive in Siwa during this lifetime . . . I await your orders, *effendi*."

Cornwall mumbled to himself for long seconds. "Fine!" he burst out at last. "We'll continue." Then he added, so only Matthew could hear, "But if I ever take my calipers to that one's head, you can bet I'll find his Approbative Center as shallow as one of these *wadis* we're forever stumbling through. The man doesn't give a fig for what anyone thinks of him or his ideas."

Matthew chuckled. "Wouldn't that be the sign of a person totally comfortable with himself? He knows his strengths and weaknesses and accepts them. In short—"

"A wise man?" growled Asa B. Cornwall. "We'll see."

The days passed in a succession of sameness. Matthew rose before dawn to watch the men at prayers, the breaking of camp, and the loading of camels—a process that even with repetition never took less than the expected two hours. This was followed by a nonstop march till late afternoon, the camels managing about twenty miles each day.

The route they followed was never evident to the untrained eye. The first several days beyond the Pyramids were filled with low, shifting sand dunes and a constant hot, dry wind that erased their footsteps almost as soon as they were made. Next came the *reg*. This was a gravel-covered plain stretching beyond the horizon that Matthew embraced with relief. The emotion was short-lived. The rocky debris was brittle and sharp, making any movement upon it an agony. At their first campsite on the *reg*, Matthew noticed Gin limping.

"What's the matter, boy?" Matthew worked his hands down each of the dog's legs, then examined his paws. The pads of Gin's feet were cracked and bleeding. "Poor fellow! You've been trying to keep up with Ali, but forgot you weren't born a camel!" Gin hung his head in Matthew's hands and whimpered softly, admitting his predicament. As Matthew examined another paw, Amir wandered by.

"There is trouble, *nasrani*?"

"Look here, Amir. What am I to do?"

"Ah," the cook bent low for his inspection. "Allah be praised, the trouble is not great. A little of my lamb grease and some special shoes will cure your noble animal."

By nightfall, Gin was liberally anointed and comfortably padding about in specially stitched camelskin booties, apparently quite satisfied with the solution to his problem.

But other trouble arose, and this time not only Gin, but the entire caravan, was affected. After a week upon the never-ending *reg*, Matthew noticed that his water rations were being cut dramatically. Then one morning he woke to find no tea waiting. He'd grown unaccountably partial to the curious brew, and found it hard to imagine starting the day without it. He went to consult with Hussein.

"About the tea business, Hussein—"

"*What* tea?" snapped the usually calm guide.

"Exactly. Have we used up our tea provisions?"

Hussein pointed to a sack in the process of being loaded. "There is tea enough to see us to Timbuktu, *nasrani*."

"Then why—"

Hussein pointed to another bag, this time a *guerba*, the tarred goatskin water container. "Look upon that *guerba*. Look upon all the *guerbas*. Do your eyes not see?"

Matthew looked. The once plump water bag had turned flaccid, settling hollowly in upon itself. Almost as if it were . . . empty. He spun to check the others. The look was the same. How could he not have noticed? Panic hit him. "There's no water? How can that be? How can we survive in the desert without water?"

Hussein shrugged. "I follow the route of my fathers. I study the stars by night, the sun by day. The wells are not where they have always been. Or they are empty. This *reg*—sometimes it is more deceitful than the sands." Hussein hawked to spit, but nothing came from his dry throat.

"How long . . . how long," Matthew asked, "until there is no water at all?"

"Two days," Hussein answered. "The camels can walk another three beyond that. Then they will begin to drop."

Matthew didn't want to ask the next question, but he had to. "And for us? How long is there for us?"

"We will drop long before the camels, *nasrani.*"

CHAPTER FOUR

MATTHEW SPIED SALVATION AT NOON. JUST BEYOND A low slope it spread out before the caravan like a dream in the midst of desolation: a wondrous lake! Surely no more than a few miles ahead, it filled the complete length of the horizon, and from his position atop Ali, Matthew could see the ripple of low waves being driven by the constant wind. He rubbed at his cracked and swollen lips and swallowed painfully. The half cup of tepid, tar-flavored water Amir allowed him at midmorning had barely cleared the grit from his throat. It hadn't come near to quenching his thirst. Now that thirst was raging again. But it didn't matter anymore. He could survive another hour or two of discomfort until they reached that marvelous, unbelievable lake. How he would wallow in it! No more of this polite sipping nonsense. He'd dive straight in, robes and all—

"Matthew! Hussein!"

Matthew twisted his body to grin at Cornwall's dawning excitement as he sleepily blinked his eyes wide on the extraordinary view. "Have a nice nap, sir?"

"What nap?" the doctor protested. "It's impossible to doze off on a camel. Especially with grit in every pore of one's body—worse than any medieval hairshirt!" Cornwall twitched evocatively. "But that's the least of my concerns at the moment. Do you see what I see? Is it possible?"

Matthew opened his mouth to shout a joyful *Yes*, but Hussein killed the word in his throat.

"*No.*"

It was a very definitive no.

"What do you mean?" Cornwall bleated pitifully. "I can almost taste it. How could my eyes deceive me? It looks like water. Enough to float a ship in! What else could it be?"

"A trick," Hussein replied. "The heat, the light—"

"An optical illusion?" wailed the doctor. "How could that be?"

"The desert has many tricks. The mirage by day . . . the *jinn* by night."

Matthew studied the lovely lake that seemed to be growing closer with every step of his camel. Reality was a hard pill to swallow. "Are the *jinn* as heartbreaking as this mirage?" he asked.

"Worse," Hussein gruffly replied. "The mirage plays with your thirst. The spirits, the *jinn*, play with your very sanity."

Suddenly Matthew was not looking forward to the coolness of the night.

They dined that evening on dates, flies, and another half cup of water apiece. The flies were not part of the official menu, but they appeared the moment the caravan stopped, covering everything. Matthew began with a mad jig of slaps, then noticed the stoicism of the Bedouin men. They'd experienced such a plague before. He calmed himself to the point of merely brushing them off his hands and face and providing the same service for Gin. It hardly mattered, because the swarms returned instantly. They were implacable, unchasable. The flies bit, too, leaving nasty welts on every inch of exposed flesh. But with the setting of the sun, the flies disappeared. There was a glorious ten minutes of peace before the next menace descended upon the diners.

"Mosquitoes!" yelped Cornwall. "Where in heaven's name do they hide in this godforsaken wilderness?" He smacked vigorously, impotently, then turned to Matthew. "Do you suppose Alexander had to put up with all of this to gain his horns of divinity?"

"Subtleties," Matthew replied through clenched teeth. His teeth were clenched to keep from swallowing mosquitoes on top of flies. Consume enough of them and they'd be holding a war in his stomach. He waved away another cloud of the bloodsuckers. "You wanted the subtleties, sir. What formed Alexander the Great's mind . . . what gave him his drive." He paused to sift a breath of air through his teeth. "If Alexander could survive the flies and the mosquitoes, hordes of barbarian armies probably meant nothing to him."

Having said his piece, Matthew cautiously inserted another date into his mouth and began to chew. Before he could swallow, a harrowing scream filled the night air. He spat out the date. "*Jinn?*"

Hussein unfolded himself from his usual spot across the fire in one quick, fluid motion. "Not the *jinn*. A different scourge of this country Allah has forgotten."

The small group raced to the tent of the camel drivers as the scream slowly faded. Hussein parted the flap and thrust a burning stick he'd grabbed from the fire into its blackness. "It is Mustafa." He stepped inside, bent next to the prostrate body, and removed something from beneath the man's bare foot. He held it to the small flame. "Scorpion." Hussein spat and consigned the remains to the fire. "We will have one less camel driver by morning."

"A scorpion bite?" Cornwall, suddenly enthusiastic, pressed his way into the closeness of the tent to kneel before the writhing man. "Fetch the medical kit, Matthew. Immediately. Here's my golden opportunity to learn if the methods described in those papyrus scrolls at the Louvre really work!" He rubbed his hands. "I could give Pliny the Elder's poultice cure a try, too!" He turned to Hussein. "Give me your knife, man. Quickly."

Matthew lingered long enough to watch in fascination as Cornwall slit the swollen welt on Mustafa's foot, then bent his head to the wound and began sucking out the venom.

"Amazing, sir!" Matthew breathed. "Who'd think to treat it like a snakebite—"

Cornwall spat blood. "Don't stand there gaping, boy. The kit!"

Matthew ran.

By morning's light Mustafa was shivering as if with fever, but he was still alive. The rest of the men treated Cornwall differently. Their veiled condescension disappeared before a new respect. Through sheer curiosity, Asa B. Cornwall had become a healer, a real doctor at last.

No one in the caravan had any desire to remain in that pest-ridden campsite a moment longer than necessary. When the packing was complete, Mustafa was unceremoniously slung across the back of a camel, and the animals plunged forward in their tethered line with something akin to enthusiasm. Or maybe it was only desperation. Matthew sat astride Ali watching the camel's nostrils twitch in a new way. He glanced down at Gin.

"Do you suppose Ali is searching for water like the rest of us, Gin?"

The dog, who'd shared Matthew's miserable water ration that morning, looked up at his master and gave a dry bark. That worried Matthew even more. If Gin began to lose his strength, he'd have to be carried slung atop the saddle, like Mustafa, only with Matthew caring for him. It would be harder for Ali. Alternately, Matthew could switch to one of the fresher relief animals. But that was almost inconceivable. The same rapport just did not exist between himself and the other camels.

Matthew bent to stroke Ali's neck, shifting his weight on the hump beneath him. The motion stopped him. Was it possible Ali's hump had shrunken overnight? Its solid buoyancy was gone. He wiggled on the saddle to verify his observation. "Definitely less hump," he mumbled. The camel's reserves were being consumed, too. And there was nothing new on the horizon but more *reg*.

Matthew peered ahead hopelessly. Then he bolted upright. Could it be?

"Hussein!"

"Nasrani?" The guide's tone had a certain quality of despair about it.

"Off to the west, northwest. Something looks different."

"It is the end of the *reg*."

"But that's wonderful!"

"It is also the beginning of the Qattara." Hussein shrugged. "The finish to one hell, the start of another."

"But water," Matthew tried. "Will there be water in this Qattara?"

"There will be mountains. And rocks like you have never seen. Rocks made by *jinn*. And caves.

As for water—" Hussein shrugged again. "Rain has not come to the Qattara in living memory."

Matthew shivered through the blistering heat. "Must we go there?"

"Siwa is beyond."

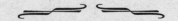

The camels stumbled on. Matthew clung to Ali with all the strength left in him. He felt himself weakening fast as the hours passed. Occasionally he raised his eyes to peer into the distance. He'd learned to rub charcoal from the cooking fires on his cheekbones and below his lashes each morning; learned how to make his eyes into slits—all to cut the sun's merciless glare. He'd learned much about the desert. Most of all he'd learned that he was probably going to die in it.

He and Doctor Cornwall and Gin would die. Amir and Mustafa and the other men—even Hussein—would die as well. The sun and the wind would leach the final moisture from their bodies and they would become nothing but dry bones littering the Sahara. All because of Dr. ABC's wild-goose chase after Alexander the Great.

Matthew shut his eyes to the eternal glare and considered the hopeless situation. Did he blame the doctor? . . . Not really. What was life without a quest? His only regret was that he wouldn't live longer. Long enough for more quests. Quests that would find the answers to changing the world, because Cornwall truly believed that what they learned from his expeditions *could* change the world. Could make it a better place. He wasn't just a silly, plump, balding phrenologist. Beneath his uninspiring façade, Asa B. Cornwall was a man of vision and drive. Like Alexander the Great himself. It was just different worlds the two had been trying to conquer.

Matthew's affection for his master, his teacher, his friend—for the doctor who had so competently dealt with the scorpion crisis only last night—grew till his chest tightened with the emotion. He turned to say something kind. Something that would give Asa B. Cornwall heart before it was too late. To say the words he'd never had the chance to say to his dying family—

"Doctor!"

Cornwall was slumped over Fatima's neck, head lolling, arms splayed.

"Hussein!" Matthew choked out. "We've got to stop! We've got to help Dr. Cornwall!"

But Hussein wasn't listening. Matthew watched as the guide, suddenly alert, pulled a dagger from

45

beneath his robes. With one efficient chop, the man sliced the rope connecting his camel to the train following. Then he kicked his mount and went loping off into the distance, toward the hard, jagged mountains of the Qattara, toward—

Matthew stiffened on his saddle. He squinted fiercely at the remote crags in the distance. There was something waiting in the foothills that seemed slightly out of place. Something just a little different from the usual mounds of rubble stone and scree. . . .

"A well!" All around him the hoarse shout rose from strained throats.

"Water!"

Belled harnesses jangled as every camel lifted its head. Ali picked up his pace, while behind Matthew, Cornwall managed a croak.

"Water? God bless us all. Did someone say *water*?"

"Yes, sir!" Matthew replied. Then he felt a curious sensation, as if his heart were dropping into his stomach. "Unless it's another false alarm. Another dry well."

But Ali apparently believed otherwise. He trotted off in pursuit of Hussein's mount, dragging the caravan behind him. In short order a roped bucket was being lowered into the questionable hole. Water came forth.

"Hamdullah." When his turn arrived, Matthew broke his enforced silence in Arabic. Then he sluiced another gourdful of water over his head and repeated the word. *"Hamdullah."* It was a good word. Absolutely the right one. God was God in any language, and Matthew was overjoyed to give praise where it was due. The murmurings around him repeated the thanks again and again. And then it was time to unload the camels and give them their share of the blessing.

The watering went on long into the night. Matthew took his turn at dropping the big leather bucket more than thirty feet through the mouth of the stone well into the depths of the desert floor. Then he laboriously hauled the rope hand over hand till the sloshing bucket could be spilled into a trough for the waiting animals. It was such an insignificant-looking thing, this well. Not much more than several yards in circumference, it could have been missed so easily. But Hussein had not missed it. Matthew pulled at the rope, thanking God once again.

Slowly his normal perspective returned. Long before the bucket reached the lip, the prayers in Matthew's mind were replaced with a new image: pulleys. How incredibly useful a block and tackle with two pulleys would be for hauling up the water. Pulleys sped through Matthew's mind until at last he tipped the water into the trough and handed the bucket to the next man. Then he stood, rubbing his strained muscles, wondering anew. This time it was over the quantity of water camels were capable of drinking. He watched one animal after another take its turn. Those still waiting filled the night sky with their groans of impatience. And when Ali's chance came at last, it almost seemed as if Matthew could see the camel's hump expanding and solidifying before his very eyes.

"Keep drinking, Ali. There's still a lot of desert ahead of us."

"Very true, *nasrani*." Hussein walked up to Ali and gave him an unexpectedly fond pat on his rump. Ali was too busy drinking to snap. "But tomorrow we rest. We will need to regain our strength for what lies ahead."

"The Qattara?" Matthew asked.

"The Qattara—and its *jinn*."

Matthew found it necessary to drink another quart of water to chase the new queasiness from his stomach.

CHAPTER FIVE

THE QATTARA WAS ANOTHER WORLD. OR MAYBE THE moon. Matthew's thoughts ran as wild as the landscape. Maybe the entire caravan had been scooped up by *jinn* in the middle of the silent desert night and plunked down on the moon. But wouldn't it be cold? And would it have this never-ending wind? Matthew reached for his water gourd and splashed some liquid into his mouth. There was enough water now, to be sure. But it seemed to evaporate from his throat as soon as he swallowed.

He felt dry as paper, as if he could be crinkled into a ball. Crinkled and tossed aside into one of the canyons bisecting the narrow passage they'd been descending through sheer cliffs since they'd left the *reg*. When Hussein finally halted the caravan for their first night in the Qattara, Matthew wanted nothing more than to retreat to one of the shadowed caves whose mouths gaped on every side. He wanted to hide from the wind and the sun; to find a complete silence.

"Dr. Cornwall?"

Asa B. Cornwall was by now capable of dismounting under his own steam, and he was standing next to his camel, Fatima, alternately pouring water down his own throat, and sprinkling the camel's head.

"What are you doing, sir?"

"Anointing Fatima, lad. She's an amazing creature, I've come to believe." He bent to pat her nose and the camel licked his hand. Cornwall beamed. "I've been seriously contemplating unpacking my craniometer and doing a few measurements of her skull. Figure out how she endures so well. But I thought I'd wash some of the dust of the road off her first—"

"Sir." Matthew gently pulled Cornwall away from the camel. "I think maybe you've had a little too much sun today. Let me get you comfortable in the shade. You can rest while I do some exploring."

"Explore? In this maze? By yourself?"

"You want to come with me?"

"After the whole day? The entire past several weeks? Surely you jest, lad!"

After Matthew had carefully checked crevices for hidden scorpions, Cornwall allowed himself to be settled within a rocky overhang. Soon he was nodding off. Matthew stood protectively over the man for a long moment. Then he shook his head and strode toward the nearest gap in the cliffs surrounding them.

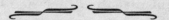

The first and most accessible cave was a disappointment. Its interior had been hollowed out only a few feet. Matthew pulled away from the opening and stood back to assess the wall of rock towering over him. If he were to scale it just a dozen yards or so there might be other openings, more interesting caves above. Just interesting enough to take his mind off the doctor's upsetting behavior, to find some solitude from his other caravan companions. If nothing else, to capture the view from above. He made a try for it, but shortly discovered that sandals were not designed with rock climbing in mind. He removed them to make the attempt barefoot.

"Yipes!"

Matthew dropped the six feet back to earth. The wall of rock was still lit—and heated—by the afternoon sun. Digging in for toeholds with his bare feet was akin to walking across burning coals. He turned to find Amir the cook watching him.

"What is this you do, *nasrani*?"

"I mean to climb this rock, Amir."

"Why?"

"To see what's on the other side."

Amir shook his head. "Only more of the same, *nasrani*. Except that the other side belongs to the *jinn*. You will displease them."

"Nonsense." Matthew was already rooting through his pannier, recently unloaded from Ali. "There!" He smiled with satisfaction. "My boots. They'll do the trick."

"Trick?" Amir stepped back. "You mean to play tricks on the *jinn*?"

"I mean to play tricks on no one, Amir. And this *jinn* business is only a silly superstition. I just need a little exercise. I've been doing nothing but riding for days!"

Amir retreated another pace, holding a protective hand before his face. *"Yak, balak!"*

Forgetting himself, Matthew responded, "No

evil will come to me, Amir. But thanks for the thought all the same." His boots firmly knotted, Matthew set off once more for his explorations.

The first twenty feet were easy. After that, Matthew had to concentrate hard for his holds. Sixty feet above the camp, he rested on a ledge and glanced down. It was a sheer fall to solid bedrock below, but the height didn't bother him. Instead it filled him with exuberance. The sort of exuberance he hadn't felt since the last time he juggled with the torches back on the boulevard du Crime. He balanced in his niche, remembering Étienne. How his acrobat friend would enjoy this climb! Remembering the countess. Then his mind soared from Paris over the Mediterranean to Nathalie. Was she still locked in her ivory tower in Cairo? Wouldn't it be lovely to have her beside him now, to show her the world spread out in all directions—

"Nasrani!"

Another bubble burst. This time it was Hussein doing the bursting.

"Descend at once! . . . I order this!"

Hussein's voice floated up with the wind like the wings of a hawk. Matthew made an instant decision to ignore the summons. He continued his climb. Another thirty feet, and he attained the rough outcropping of the cliff's summit. He lunged over the top, paused to give a wave to the camp below, then turned to find yet another world.

It was no longer the moon. Perhaps this was another planet. The valley opening before him was peopled with giants! Matthew whistled long and low.

"Not giants," he murmured, "but near enough to."

Hundreds of pillars of rock writhed and twisted toward and away from each other in an ungainly dance that continued far into the distance. The sun colored them with reds and pinks—even greens and blues. It was the most color Matthew had yet seen in the desert. He covered the few yards to the far edge of his narrow peak to get a better view, then found a steplike path down, cleft by nature into the very cliff side itself. He descended a few feet, eyes still focused on the pillars, when the sun's rays shifted slightly, illuminating and drawing his attention to the wall beside him. Knees buckling, Matthew sat.

"I don't believe this!"

Etched into the wall beside him were animals. He stretched a finger to touch the designs. "Giraffes," he whispered. Huge giraffes towered over him, nearly half their true size. "Elephants and deer." He followed the trunk of an elephant down to the next step. . . . "An odd sort of bird." It had a very long, ungainly neck perched atop a fat, feathered body and stood balanced on spindly legs. . . . "And people!" Not people as in a proper painting. More like scarecrow people, drawn like sticks. Lots of them. They were chasing after a horned rhinoceros with spears in their hands.

Matthew traveled halfway down the far side of his cliff until the etchings and the sun gave out at the same time. He glanced up and saw the darkness coming. It would arrive soon and with an awful suddenness. He scrambled back up the steps.

"There were pictures of people, I tell you!" Matthew was trying to explain his experience to the dubious men during dinner. "And that bird—"

"An ostrich, from your description, Matthew," Dr. Cornwall offered. His mind was sharp again after his nap. "The Boers have described them in South Africa. Huge, awkward, nonflying birds almost eight feet tall, by all accounts. But there couldn't have been giraffes and elephants—not to mention these other creatures—anywhere near the Sahara for more than ten thousand years!"

Matthew looked up from the flickering flames of the campfire. "What does it all mean, sir?"

"It means the Sahara wasn't always dry, lad. People once lived here—"

"It means only more work of the *jinn*," growled Hussein, still in a snit over Matthew's disobedience. As if to prove his point, wild laughter abruptly echoed down the canyons of rock through the darkness surrounding them. Evil laughter. Hussein nodded almost approvingly.

"Hyenas," Cornwall proclaimed. "Leo Africanus mentioned them in his sixteenth-century history of the Sahara. Called them abject and silly creatures."

The wicked sound repeated itself. Instead of remaining companionably about the fire telling stories, as they'd taken to doing after the evening meal, one by one the men slunk off to their tents, swords hefted in protection.

"Hyenas?" Matthew asked. "But we've seen no animals at all this far—"

"Nocturnal creatures," Cornwall amplified. "They live on carrion."

"What carrion?"

"Maybe us," Hussein muttered as he joined his men.

"I do appreciate Hussein's consistency,"

Cornwall chuckled. "The man's a pessimist through and through." He tossed a forgotten twig on the fire and settled back to enjoy the night.

Matthew looked upon the hard rock of the Qattara with new eyes the next morning. He'd slept well the night before—slept well despite the constant hysterical laughter of the hyena and the howls of something else that Cornwall had also named before they'd left the embers of the fire for their tent: the Saharan cheetah. There was something marvelous about giving a name to the unknown. With the naming, the terrors disappeared. Every Arab and Bedouin in their party had staggered from his tent bleary-eyed and wan from the same night's entertainment. But for Matthew, the *jinn* had ceased to exist. What he wanted now was to find more of the incredible messages left by a forgotten people.

Matthew spent the next several days of the journey atop Ali staring hard at every foot of smooth-walled rock they passed. He stared so hard he became dizzy from the effort. But there weren't pictures in plain sight for anyone passing to see.

He developed a theory that perhaps these images had been hidden by their makers on purpose—for what purpose he wasn't sure. But as soon as the day's halt was called he went exploring again, poking into nooks and crannies, clambering over boulders, and climbing megaliths and cliffs. When Hussein and the other men saw him setting off, they made the automatic sign against evil, but they gave up their attempts to stop him.

It was during the afternoon of his third day of searching that Matthew made his next discovery. It was also by chance. In fact, it was made through clumsiness. He'd forced his way through the tight space between a group of monolithic stone towers, staggered into an unexpected opening beyond, and landed flat on his face. Nose to the gravel and dirt, he sighed, when something caught his attention at ground level.

"What in the world . . ."

Matthew inched closer, propped himself on an elbow, and examined the pile of debris before him: fractured bones; bits of charcoal; something else, too. He delicately extricated a fragment of shaped stone from the rubble, then sat up to examine it more closely. It was flint. An arrowhead! He dove back into the pile and soon had several more shaped stones before him. He fingered the carefully hewn edges, feeling the sharpness. Images of people crafting these tools swam before him. He could almost see them sitting around this very hearth, chipping usefulness into the stone. Then they would be ready for the hunt. Off they'd go to lie in wait for a herd of grazing deer, or one of those ostriches.

This closed circle of stone he'd stumbled into was the campsite of ancient people. There was no question in Matthew's mind. What else had they left behind? His eyes traveled up the smooth insides of the monoliths. Here were his pictures again. But this time they were different. Rather than being lightly etched into the rock, these images had been carved. Animals and people stood out boldly in a long bas-relief of action that completely surrounded him. And there were new animals. Hippopotami. Crocodiles. Creatures of the water in the midst of the Sahara! Dr. Cornwall must see these things.

Matthew scooped up the arrowheads and tucked them in a pocket beneath his robes. He'd run back to camp and rouse Cornwall from his afternoon nap. He'd make him come and see the site. He'd personally shove and squeeze the doctor through the tight opening. Maybe Cornwall had some drawing materials in his bag. Even just a few scraps of paper. These pictures needed to be copied. Needed to be shown to the world. They were so much more interesting than any dry old skull. Even the skull of Alexander the Great! The people carved in this rock seemed almost alive. They were different from his earlier discovery in other ways, too. These people had fuller bodies and were wearing clothes. At least, loincloths. And some kind of headdresses. . . . Matthew squinted at the line of reliefs. No, they were masks. *Cat masks.*

The discovery was entrancing. How different everything was in the desert now, yet some things were the same. Those masks could represent a cheetah, like the one heard on the prowl the last few nights. He sat back on his haunches, unable to tear himself away from the mysterious images. Why were these people wearing the masks? In honor of the huge cat? To try and capture some of the magnificent creature's strength for their own hunt? Or could there be other reasons? Reasons he would never understand?

The hairs on the back of Matthew's neck rose suddenly. Then the hairs on his arms. The very air had changed within the circle. It was charged with some kind of life, some kind of power. He froze, willing complete stillness to his body. Someone— or something—had entered the ancient space he shared with the carvings and the bones.

An eternity passed with eyes drilling into his back. Was it some ghost he'd called up by entering this long forgotten sacred place? Was it the *jinn* he'd so casually dismissed? Matthew could stand the sensation no longer. With infinite caution, he turned. And bit back his own gasp. Perhaps he'd unwittingly beckoned them all. And here they were, in the form of—

A *cheetah*!

The cat was enormous. Bigger than a leopard. Almost as big as a lion. It was terrible and beautiful. And it crouched on its haunches, inspecting him.

"Your howl is mighty, my friend," Matthew murmured. "Remind me to be frightened the next time I hear it echoing through the night."

The cat blinked. Its fur was a tawny golden color, short and sleek.

"Awed, if you prefer," Matthew added. How had the cat found its way inside the circle? There was only one opening, and that hardly large enough. Yet there it waited, all coiled energy, a wall of sheer black stone behind it, only himself before it—

The cheetah bared its fangs.

"Definitely awed," he whispered.

It sprang.

There was no time, no way to escape. Matthew

shut his eyes and prayed. He waited for the col-
lision of bodies. For the gashing of claws and the
gnashing of fangs. For the pain and oblivion.
And waited.

He opened his eyes.

He was alone.

"Hamdullah." His breath returned. "Oh, yes.
Hamdullah."

Matthew shakily rose to his feet. Had it been a
dream? He waited for his heartbeat to slow, for
the tremors running through his body to stop.
Then he studied the dust near his boots. No. Not
a dream. There were the tracks. That's where the
beast had crouched. Here was where he'd sprung.
Then nothing. Nothing at all.

Matthew shook his head in a clearing motion. He
nodded to the masked hunters surrounding him.

"You win."

He carefully retrieved the arrowheads from his
pocket and laid them out in a row before the pictures. He bowed.

"I give you peace for another ten thousand
years."

Matthew left the secret circle.

"Any new finds this afternoon?" Dr. Cornwall
inquired during dinner.

"Nothing worth mentioning," Matthew answered.

"A pity. Hussein tells me we leave the Qattara tomorrow. I was rather hoping to see some of your pictures."

"Maybe in another part of the desert, sir."

"We reach Siwa soon," Hussein announced from across the fire. "There are only a few days of the Great Sand Sea to journey through." He smiled with satisfaction. "And we will arrive." He spat out a date pit. "I think maybe we travel home a different way. Straight north, then along the coast. That way has no *jinn*—only pirates."

"Pirates!" exclaimed Cornwall. "You prefer real pirates to some fantasy of danger?"

"Yes," said Hussein.

"Hussein might have a point, sir," Matthew offered. "Hussein knows best. Has the tea finished brewing yet, Amir?"

CHAPTER SIX

THE CARAVAN WAS BACK IN THE LAND OF THE *erg*, THE
shifting sand dunes. But these dunes had little
relationship to the lower mounds they'd crossed
beyond the Pyramids of Giza. Hussein had called
this the Great Sand Sea, and now Matthew knew
why. These dunes were enormous. They were
mountains of sand that billowed on and on like
the waves of an ocean, seemingly forever. Half a
day out of the Qattara, and Cornwall's expedition was wandering between the troughs and

heights of these incredible shimmering mountains, enveloped within the alien beauty.

"Hussein," Matthew called. "How can you possibly find your way through this?"

Their guide was unperturbed. In fact, he seemed rejuvenated since leaving the Qattara and its hidden threat of *jinn*. He twisted around on his saddle to actually offer Matthew a smile, exposing tea-stained teeth. "The sand has colors, *nasrani*. It has textures. You learn to tell the good from the bad."

"How?"

Hussein shrugged. "The most famous guide of days gone by was completely blind. He would navigate by holding the sand in his hand, feeling its coarseness, sniffing its aroma—then point the way. . . . It is something born to a desert man. In his bones. You would not understand."

Matthew wanted to understand, but Hussein declined to elaborate, returning instead to his solitary cocoon. So Matthew watched the directions their guide took. He learned to distinguish between the lighter and darker shades of tan, and slowly began to perceive a pattern between the harder sands and the softer, more dangerous areas. There was a pattern to the dunes themselves, too. There were gently sloping ridges with smooth, rounded summits that looked like nothing so much as beached whales. There were cascading, pyramid-shaped sand hills. And there were the crested dunes the men called *seif*, the Arabic word for sword. They all ran in long fields precisely north to south, perpendicular to the caravan's route.

As the afternoon wore on, they approached a particularly enormous *seif*. Matthew studied its crescent shape, then absently rubbed at the scar on his cheek. He hadn't thought of the scar for months. Not since Nathalie's touch in her perfumed midnight garden. Had it been months, or only weeks? . . . Or had it been years? His entire sense of time had been skewed by this strange land. So had his sense of reality.

What incredible things he and Dr. Cornwall and Gin had survived in this chartless desert since that night under the crescent moon. He'd learned new kinds of endurance, new kinds of fear. Experiencing the desert could make even the tribulations of the body snatcher's vengeful pursuit seem insignificant. What was one man compared to a phenomenon like this?

Only a few more days and they would arrive safely in the oasis of Siwa at last. They would achieve the first part of their strange quest for Alexander the Great that had begun in Paris—or maybe on the jagged cliffs of St. Helena lifetimes ago. Only a few more days of stifling heat that seared one's very lungs with each breath taken. Only a few more days of putrid water and sand-dried dates and tea, and Ali's queasy gait as the camel climbed each succeeding dune—

"*Ula-la-la-la-la-la-la-la-la-la-la-la—*"

Matthew jerked away from his thoughts at the ululating wail. It was a sound like nothing he'd ever heard. Neither had he seen what he was seeing now. Before his eyes was a sight to freeze the very marrow in one's bones: swarming over the rim of the dune ahead were hordes of men—*blue* men! Huge blue men completely swathed from head to toe in indigo-blue robes. They sat high upon their camels and were ferocious to behold. The swords glinting in the sun were like extensions of their bodies. And those swords were closing in on Hussein and himself. On the entire caravan. The ululating cry continued. Matthew strongly suspected that the intentions of these blue men were neither honorable nor pacific.

Battle raged around Matthew and Dr. Cornwall, the only two among their party who were unarmed. From atop Ali, the deceitful air and light of the desert played games with Matthew's perception. His ears were filled with Ali's nervous groans, Gin's howls, and men's shrieks. His eyes seemed to be seeing the action of the raiders in slow motion. The assault of the blue men proceeded in a dream of scattered sand: the wild onslaught; Hussein's guards tardily pulling curved swords from their shoulders; blades being raised; blades slicing down; red blood coloring golden sands; men on their knees, alternately begging and praying; swords rising again.

No mercy.

Then it was Matthew's turn, and Asa B. Cornwall's.

Matthew was swept to the sand with one blow. Blue hands ripped off his turban. Blue fingers hauled him to his knees by his hair. A sword still dripping redly hovered above him—

"Stop!"

The bloody dream changed to real time. Matthew looked up. The voice belonged to the largest of the veiled blue men—their leader, their sheik.

"See his mark." The voice was harsh and guttural, coming from deep within the seven-foot frame. "It is the crescent moon of Mohammed himself. Spare him."

Hamdullah. Matthew bent his head to the sand in the gesture of prayer and thanks he'd watched Hussein and Amir and Mustafa and the others perform every morning and evening of their journey. Hussein and Amir and Mustafa. All gone now, forever. His throat tightened. He raised his head to search for Dr. Cornwall. Was it possible he was still alive? . . . Yes, but not for much longer. There, next to his camel, the doctor knelt under a sword ready to sever his quivering head.

"Stop!" Matthew roared the same Arabic word. "He is a sorcerer! A *Maghribi*! A healer, also. Dead, he will call disaster upon you. Alive, he will bring you much luck!" He stared boldly up into the eyes of the sheik. It was all of the veiled face that was visible. And those eyes were black and cold. Matthew held his breath as the eyes glinted, then watched the blue hand rise to signal a halt. The raider above Cornwall hesitated, then lowered his sword, leaving Cornwall to disintegrate into a puddle of jelly upon the sands.

"Prove this thing—"

Matthew's attention shot back to the leader.

"—and you will live to be a slave. You and the old man. If not, you will join your comrades."

Slave, or dead? The decision was easy. Matthew made a motion begging leave to rise. Permission was granted.

"Dr. Cornwall?" He stumbled on rubbery legs the few yards to his friend and knelt next to him.

"Sir. You've got to pull yourself together. Where have you packed your calipers and craniometer?"

"Calipers?" Cornwall mumbled. "Craniometer?"

Matthew grabbed his master by the shoulders and shook. Cornwall's body lolled like a rag doll. "Come on, Doctor. Don't let me down. Don't let either of us down. You're about to give the performance of your life. For your life."

"But Hussein . . . the guards . . ."

"Dead, sir. Every last one of them. Slaughtered trying to defend us. If you want your bones to join theirs—"

Cornwall snapped back to alertness. "No, no. That won't be necessary." He staggered upright and began dusting sand from his robes. "The instruments are packed in my satchel, inside Fatima's pannier."

Matthew turned to the leader. "He needs his magic tools. May I get them?"

"Later," the sheik pronounced. "When the labor is finished."

The sun set before Cornwall was given his opportunity to save his life. The blue men had decided to camp just beyond the crown of the *seif* that had hidden their dastardly ambush, leaving the scene of carnage behind them.

Matthew was ordered to do the final dirty work:
to strip the bodies of his friends naked in search
of any hidden valuables the blue men might
desire. It was one of the saddest tasks he'd ever
had to perform.

"Ibrahim," he murmured, turning over a body.
"You were kinder than most to the camels. . . .
Mustafa. Dr. Cornwall couldn't save your life a
second time. . . . Amir." He stopped to swipe at his
eyes. "Amir. You loved Gin. You were a friend to
me. And you made fine tea."

Matthew worked his way through the scattered
bodies, collecting their robes and pitifully few
personal possessions, then doing his best to cover
them with sand. He knew the protection would
not last long. The desert winds would soon expose
the bodies to the merciless sun of another day, of
endless days to come. But the small gesture of
respect gave him some comfort.

Then he came to the final body. This was the
one he'd been studiously avoiding, trying to post-
pone the inevitable. It was inconceivable to him
that Hussein could truly be dead. How could their
proud, wise, feisty little guide be dead? Matthew
turned the body over tenderly, reached to wipe
the sand from the man's eyes a final time—

"I see you, *nasrani*."

Matthew jumped back. "Hussein! You're

alive!" He retreated another foot. "Or is it *jinn* deceiving me?"

"So, you believe at last?" came the dry whisper.

"Oh, yes. I believe." Matthew crept closer. "But how could you be alive? The blood—"

"Is that of my camel." Hussein stirred himself to half rise on an elbow. It was a painful process. "But my head is not well. The hilt of a Tuareg sword struck me a mighty blow. I could fight no more." He fingered his swollen brow. "Then forgetfulness overwhelmed all until you came."

"Is that who these blue men are? Tuareg?"

Hussein nodded, wincing with the effort. "The most feared raiders of the desert. They live by pillage and trade in forbidden things. . . ." He closed his eyes a long moment. "Gold, ivory . . . but above all human beings. Slaves." Hussein fell back onto the sand.

"Hussein," Matthew begged. "Don't leave us now! Dr. Cornwall and I alone have been spared—but only for the moment."

"I am as good as dead anyway," mumbled Hussein. "The Tuareg will never take me with them. They want only the camels and their loads. Prisoners are too much trouble if they are not the black men desired by the slave trade—or the occasional healthy infidel."

"Here." Matthew reached for his water gourd.

He uncorked it and held it to Hussein's lips. "Drink while I plan. My master has his own life yet to save. I think it will be the evening's entertainment. . . . If he succeeds, we can beg a favor—"

"What favor can you ask of the blue men?"

Matthew gently set down Hussein's head. "Your life." He corked the gourd, leaving it beside the guide. Next he gathered his sack of booty. "Lie here and rest. I'll return for you before morning, Allah willing."

Hussein gave one of his old shrugs. *"Kismet."* He sighed. "I will receive my portion as fate wills."

"Fate has nothing to do with it," Matthew growled. "But Dr. Asa B. Cornwall does."

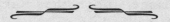

The night sky was filled with a million stars, but no moon. Matthew and Dr. Cornwall had been fed a bowl of camel's milk and a pasty lump of something totally indistinguishable. They ate the offerings without question or complaint. When the meal was completed, the leader of the blue men crossed his legs upon his pillow of office and addressed them.

"I, Sheik Ibn er-Rakik, am ready. Convince me that the old one deserves to live."

It was time to begin.

Matthew realized that, to succeed, Dr. Cornwall's

performance required three things: light, ritual, and a sense of mystery. Light was perhaps the most difficult of these requirements. He'd been puzzling over the solution since clearing the killing field. Now he spoke to the sheik.

"May I be allowed to complete preparations for the great magic?"

Ibn er-Rakik nodded magisterially. While his men settled at a suitable distance to watch, Matthew fetched his props. Wood was the great problem of the desert. There was none. He'd had to gather the slats of broken camel saddles, find Amir's supply of lamb grease, and cobble together torches. Now he approached the small fire of dry camel-thorn that Rakik sat beside and carefully lit and buried a torch to either side of the leader. He glanced back at the doctor, fidgeting with his equipment. "Are you ready, sir?"

"As ready as I'll ever be. Although I must say, I usually have better results with live heads when my subjects are women—"

"Rakik is veiled, Doctor. That will have to be inspiration enough."

Cornwall snorted. "About that bloody veil and headdress. How am I supposed to take my measurements with yards of cloth in the road?"

"Improvise, sir. You saw how attached these

Tuareg are to their cloth. They wouldn't remove it even for eating."

"Improvise! I've never improvised on science in my life! Phrenology is sacred to me, Matthew Morrissey—"

"So is your life, I hope. If you can't improvise, lie. Just make it dramatic. For both our sakes."

"What is being said?" barked Rakik.

"Nothing of import, O Great Sheik."

No more interruptions. They'd have to start the performance. Matthew thrust his remaining three unlit torches into the fire, praying he was skillful enough to handle the unmatched weights. As he began to juggle the flames, he made his introductions in Arabic.

"The all-mighty Asa B. Cornwall hides many things within his simple form. He is a sorcerer of power and strength in faraway lands. Tonight—as a sign of utmost respect—he reveals to you his secret name. It is a name that carries enormous potency."

Matthew paused in his commentary for a sign of interest from Rakik. He received it in one raised eyebrow. The torches spun higher into the sky, flaring up to the stars.

"The name—oh, cringe with fear, all you who hear this secret—the name is . . . *Dr. ABC!*"

A soft sigh rose from the men gathered in the shadows.

"The name signifies the beginning of the alphabet, the beginning of words, the beginning of all knowledge known to man . . ."

Matthew madly embroidered his introduction, suspecting that style was more important than the content itself. He'd listened to Hussein's men tell tales around their own night fires. Long yarns of Scheherazade and the thousand and one nights of endless stories that kept her alive. He'd have to develop some of that same ability if he and Dr. Cornwall were to survive this night.

His torches wheeled into the sky, floated back, were captured, and released again. *Resurrection.* He needed it now more than ever.

". . . And now Dr. ABC will share this knowledge with you. With you, alone, Ibn er-Rakik, because you are the mightiest of desert sheiks. You are the scourge of infidels, the pillager of both high and low. You are a god among men, because you bring unto man a gift only a god can bestow—the gift of death."

Matthew glanced through the flames to note how Rakik was taking his exorbitant flattery. Apparently well. The villain was nodding with pleasure behind his veil.

"But," Matthew continued, "as the giver of death, as the messenger who sends so many men to the Gardens of Paradise, you can also bestow another gift when you choose. Only if you choose." Matthew caught first one torch, then another. He blew them out. He snatched the third torch from the sky, brought it to his mouth, swallowed, then spewed the flame—the great flame the countess had loved enough to bestow gold upon its giver—toward Rakik.

The tongue of fire shot so close to Rakik, Matthew thought his veil might ignite. He held his breath. The flame hesitated a hairsbreadth from disaster before dissolving into the night. Rakik never flinched. Matthew gasped for air to refill his lungs. He finished his piece.

"Choose the gift of life, O Greatest of Sheiks. For sweet though the Gardens of Paradise be, there is also sweetness to be found in living under these stars." Matthew bowed.

"Dr. ABC will now approach to perform his greatest magic upon you. It is not the magic of illusions, which any fakir could perform. Oh, no . . . it is something much greater. It is the magic that will open your mind that you may truly know yourself."

"Masterly, lad," Cornwall whispered as he neared the sheik with his phrenological tools held high. "Didn't understand a word, but the presentation was masterly. If I don't survive the night, remember that I'm proud of you. As proud as any father for his only son."

Warmth spread through Matthew as he bowed again, this time in respect and love for Asa B. Cornwall. "Thank you, sir. I'll remember."

Now Dr. ABC stood poised before the sheik. Taking a lesson from Matthew's dramatics, he raised his craniometer and calipers to the stars in offering. Next he set aside the calipers to run the craniometer's glinting silver through the flames of each torch in turn. Finally he suspended the instrument over Ibn er-Rakik's turbaned head. "I ought to tighten the screws," he intoned, "till I squeeze the brains from your ugly skull, you sorry excuse for a human being, you caveman—"

Matthew took his cue. "Man of the caves," he chanted. "You who were birthed in the sacred confines of the Qattara, with *jinn* blessing your arrival. O, you ancient one of beetled brow and strength of ten. You who are the forebear of the mighty sheik Ibn er-Rakik, inspire Dr. ABC with his analysis. Give Dr. ABC the power to make Ibn er-Rakik understand the innermost thoughts that emanate from his broad and low skull, a skull worthy to be counted as brother to the fabled body snatcher himself—"

Cornwall lowered the craniometer and gently

screwed it to Rakik's headdress. He squinted through the flickering light. "Base of the brain d to e, f over f. . ." Through the hushed silence of the desert night, Asa B. Cornwall charted Rakik's lumpy turban.

CHAPTER SEVEN

"WAKE UP, HUSSEIN!"

Hussein groaned and rolled onto his back. His eyes blinked open to the fading stars, then to Matthew. "*Nasrani* . . . by the beard of the Prophet! You have returned as you promised! With my life, or—"

Matthew grinned. "With your life. But—"

The guide struggled to a sitting position. "I fear this *but*. Explain."

Matthew's grin spread. "*But* you have been

consigned as personal slave to the great Dr. Cornwall."

Hussein hacked and spat. "So nothing changes after all."

Laughter bubbled up from Matthew's chest. "You may be right. Here—" He offered his arm. "Let me help you over the dune into the land of the living."

Hussein accepted the assistance, but only as far as the rim of the *seif*. There he shrugged away from Matthew and entered the Tuareg camp on his own two feet, as cocky as ever.

Sheik Ibn er-Rakik lounged on his embroidered pillow during breakfast. On a small, brightly colored rug next to him sat Gin, tethered securely by his side. Rakik carefully filled a bowl with camel's milk and offered it to the dog. Matthew, sitting cross-legged in the sand between Cornwall and Hussein, watched him lap it up.

"Traitor," he muttered.

Gin whimpered guiltily before returning to the milk. Rakik caressed the animal, then drained his own bowl. At last he set about explaining the new order of things.

"The sorcerer shall ride behind me at all times. His slave shall ride behind him. At night

the sorcerer's tent will be raised next to my own.
You—" He stabbed a finger toward Matthew.
"You and the holy *Maghribi*'s slave will sleep
outside his tent flap to protect him. And," he
concluded, "his secret name shall not be spoken,
upon pain of death." Rakik carefully selected several of those odd, pasty balls of food from the
brass platter placed before him. He tossed one to
Gin, who snapped it up, and pressed the other
on the doctor.

"What's he saying?" Cornwall asked. "And
what is this foul concoction? It's the third one
he's made me eat."

"Ground locust meal," Hussein explained.
"Moistened with soured camel's milk. A staple of
the Tuareg diet. Very healthy."

"Bugs?" choked Cornwall. He blanched. "I'm
eating *bugs*?"

"And you will continue eating them," Matthew
broke in. "With a polite smile and even a *Hamdullah*
thrown in for good measure . . . if you choose to
remain the apple of Rakik's eye. He's saying you
are to be his shadow. His *protected* shadow."

"After the analysis I made of him last night?"

"Remember that I interpreted that analysis,
sir."

"True. I wish I could have understood even a
little of what you were saying." Cornwall forced a

nod at Rakik, whispered a plaintive *"Hamdullah,"* and bit into his locust treat. After a moment he regained control again. "But oddly enough, Matthew, even wrapped as it was, I could tell the man's head was not broad and low. It's actually quite aristocratic in shape. I suspect vastly enlarged organs of Acquisitiveness and Destructiveness beneath all that blue cloth, though."

"It's common sense, sir," Matthew said. "Phrenology does seem to be based on common sense. Not all brutality is mindless, as was the case with our body snatcher."

"How perspicacious of you, lad. I suppose I suspected, but never truly *believed* that evil could be rooted in intelligence gone bad. I must reread Milton's *Paradise Lost* at first opportunity—"

"Silence!" growled Rakik. "You—" He pointed at Matthew again. "I could order chains set upon your neck and ankles and force you to march, but we have camels enough and they need tending. You will work with my men until we meet the caravan from Timbuktu." He gave Matthew an assessing stare. "If I keep you healthy, you will bring more gold from its slave master."

This was not news—neither the fact of slavery, nor his possible price. It only verified Hussein's comments about the desirability of white slaves.

There wasn't much point in worrying about any of it now. Survive one day at a time. Matthew rose with dispatch and bowed. "I thank you for your consideration, O Great Sheik." Turning, he ran smack into a vast blue man who grabbed him bodily and tossed him toward the nearest camel. The honeymoon was over.

By the time they were en route for the day at last, Matthew began to truly understand the new order of things. He sat slumped in exhaustion on an anonymous camel near the rear of the caravan. Not only was the view not as fine as from the front, but as the wind rose, he found himself nearly overcome with dust and odors from the progress of several hundred camels in front of him. He stretched his aching muscles. He wasn't used to hard labor, either. Loading camels was the least of it. Much harder was urging recalcitrant animals to rise, then being kicked and whipped by the Tuareg when he refused to use the same violence on the poor beasts of burden.

Matthew groaned a groan worthy of a camel. He knew now why they bit. With all his bruises settling in, he was ready to bite his keepers, too. These men enjoyed giving blows.

Was there any way to improve his situation?

Only in the little things, he was certain. He began by rewinding his turban cloth Tuareg style: ends wrapped around his nose and mouth, giving him some protection from the dust. If the cloth were blue instead of white, he'd look like one of the raiders himself. That done, he squinted ahead the long distance to the front of the line. Rakik was leading, followed by Cornwall, as ordered. Behind the doctor rode Hussein. Matthew grinned in spite of his discomfort. Not only was Hussein the slave to Cornwall, but he'd been made keeper of the noble dog Gin, too. That meant the dog was enthroned on the saddle in front of Hussein. Now Gin squirmed miserably atop Ali, wanting nothing more than to run freely by the side of his friend. Even Gin had been enslaved to Sheik Ibn er-Rakik.

Little improved by the end of the long, sizzling day. Dazed from the incredible glare of endless dunes, Matthew dismounted from his camel and walked forward just in time to watch Cornwall do the same. But the doctor achieved his solid footing in an entirely novel way. Fatima was already halfway to her knees and Cornwall preparing himself for his usual bumbling descent when the sheik ordered, "Wait!"

Unsure of what to do, Cornwall froze.

"The slave of the great sorcerer will assist him in dismounting," Rakik clarified.

Hussein glanced over in disbelief. He'd had his hands full dumping Gin from Ali's back, and now the camel—obviously blaming Hussein for the dog's long hours of unhappiness—made a mighty lunge with his neck, giving Hussein a great *thwack* before catching the man firmly by the thigh.

"Son of the devil himself!" Hussein slapped at the camel's mouth, trying to dislodge his large yellow teeth. "You will pay for this!"

Matthew arrived in time to stroke Ali's neck and whisper in his ear. "Enough of this, my friend. You're picking the wrong enemy. Set your sights on Rakik, instead."

As if he understood, Ali loosened his grip and swung his neck to eye the blue man, giving Hussein the chance to limp away. But the guide's ordeal was not over. Rakik, now dismounted himself, poked Hussein in the stomach with the hilt of his whip.

"Down, slave. Prostrate yourself so your master may dismount."

Cornwall finally caught the gist of the action, and protested loudly. "My good sheik, that won't be necessary, not necessary at all—"

"The mighty sorcerer," Matthew tried translating, "would prefer to dismount by himself."

His words were ignored. Rakik shoved a foot at Hussein's back, and the hapless man landed face first in the sand. Cornwall gave Matthew a beleaguered look, then attempted to use his human stepping-stone as gently as possible. Rakik nodded once and strode away.

Matthew gave Hussein a hand up. "Are you all right?"

Hussein spat sand and muttered darkly, but before Matthew could offer further support, another huge blue man bore down on him.

"You. Unload the camels."

Matthew sighed. Another two hours of work. Maybe three or four, taking into account the stolen camels whose keepers were all dead. The sigh cost him a sharp lash across the shoulders from the Tuareg's whip. Smarting, he trotted toward the baggage animals. He'd have to learn to move first and complain afterward.

<hr/>

The night brought little rest. Matthew and Hussein huddled outside the flaps of Cornwall's tent, trying to find warmth in their thin robes as the temperature dropped.

"Perhaps you should have left me behind that dune," Hussein said. "Left me to meet my fate."

Matthew shivered in concert with the guide.

"Nonsense," he said. But his heart wasn't completely in the protest. "Things have got to improve."

"They could also get worse," Hussein pointed out. Then he added, *"nasrani."*

Matthew glanced at the man. Hussein's *nasrani* was no longer spoken as an insult. In some indefinable way, the word now sounded like *friend*. In spite of himself, Matthew smiled into the cold night. Emboldened, he snatched at Cornwall's tent flap and drew it around his friend and himself. Together they listened to the doctor's snores until Hussein began adding his drone to the night music. Matthew's shivering slowed and soon his own eyes closed.

On the fifth day of their captivity something changed. Rakik's caravan had been plowing through the great dunes in a steady west-southwest direction, taking them farther and farther from the safety of Siwa, farther and farther into the endless sea of sand. About noon, Matthew woke from a heavy doze of exhaustion to glance over his camel's neck. He rubbed at his eyes, not believing what he saw. Then looked again.

An odd thing was happening to the sand. It seemed to be rising from the surface of the dunes.

In fact, the dunes themselves appeared to be ascending, almost levitating. He watched as the entire horizon ahead rose a yard, two yards, more . . . and with the rising, the usual crisp, clear blue heavens also changed. Before Matthew's eyes the sand formed itself into a red and brown cloud. As he stared, incapable of anything but wonder, the giant windblown cloud grew larger and larger . . . seemed about to obliterate the very sky—

"Storm!" yelled the rider ahead of him.

Matthew peered up the long line of the caravan. At its head, Rakik had his arm raised. He was calling a halt. In the middle of the day?

From that moment there was no more time for wonder. No time for explanations, either. Everything and everyone moved too quickly. The camels were hustled into a wide double circle. Even before unloading, they were hobbled. Men worked like dervishes to erect tents within this circle of shelter. Wind rose to near-hurricane force, sending sand cutting through every inch of exposed flesh, causing sand to bore through the very cloth of one's clothing. Matthew was forced to ignore the discomfort and the fear. The animals still needed attention. But there wasn't enough time to unload them all before the sandstorm was atop the caravan. As visibility was cut to a few inches, the blue men disappeared into their shelters. No one noticed or cared when Matthew and Hussein stumbled into Cornwall's tent for refuge.

———————

Matthew leaned against the tent wall, fighting for breath. As the airborne sand settled to the floor, he began to make out the forms of Cornwall and Hussein through the haze. He tore off his turban and shook pounds of sand from the cloth.

"Water," he gasped. "Did anyone think to bring some water?"

Hussein forced himself up from the pillow-shaped object he'd collapsed against. "Here."

"A *guerba*," Matthew whispered. "Thank God you found one." He crawled over to the bag and bent under the spout.

"Wait!" Hussein's fingers covered the stopper. "We must have an understanding."

"What about?" Cornwall asked. He was on his knees, second in line for a go at the precious stuff.

"Do you hear that?" Hussein's voice rose over the vicious blasts tearing around the tent.

Matthew raised his head. "The wind?"

"The wind," Hussein agreed. "It will rage for three days. If we are lucky."

"If not?" Matthew asked.

"Then it will rage for five days. The *khamaseen*,

the sandstorm of the springtime, lasts five days. Always. Then—"

Cornwall cleared his throat. His words still came out as a croak. "Then what?"

"Then it stops. As quickly as it started. But this storm . . . it began as the *ajaij*, the storm that can come at any season on the desert, making the sands rise up from the dunes."

Matthew nodded. This is what he'd seen.

"But then it became something else," Hussein continued. "Something I have never seen in the summer." He had the full attention of his audience. He continued. "I cannot say how long this storm will last. Three days. Five days. A week or more. It was such a summer sandstorm that covered an entire caravan in the time of my grandfather—"

"And?" Matthew asked, spellbound.

"And nothing of the caravan was ever seen again."

Cornwall tried his voice once more. This time it was a squeak. "So we ration the water."

"Yes," Hussein verified. "We ration the food, also."

"You brought food, too?" Matthew asked. "When? How?"

"While you were tending the camels," Hussein answered.

91

"Please, don't let it be locusts!" Asa B. Cornwall prayed.

Hussein smiled at last and pointed to several sacks whose outlines were becoming clearer as the air continued to settle itself. "No. I took supplies only from our own pack animals. We should have dates, and olives, and dried camel meat."

"Thank heaven," Cornwall said. "But now, about that water—"

"Now, we may all share a taste of this water."

From beneath his robes Hussein pulled forth a cup. Matthew sat back and waited for his measure. If there'd been any doubt about it before, the situation—like the air—was now becoming clearer. Hussein had grasped for the upper hand and was once more in charge.

Chapter Eight

Sprawled in a bed and blanket of sand, Matthew idly raised an arm to watch the grains trickling from him like an hourglass. "If I kept my arm steady, we could tell the time," he said.

"What would be the point?" Cornwall groused. "It will end when it ends. It feels like months already."

Hussein shoved away from his section of the tent wall and shook his head, spraying more sand. "Two days. It has only been two days. There were two periods of complete darkness, and now is the morning of the third day."

Matthew dropped his arm and listened to the howling wind. It had been raging for so long that he'd almost begun to ignore it. "Gin is surely safe with Rakik, but how will the camels survive this storm, Hussein?" he wondered. "They've had no water or food, and some of the poor beasts are still loaded with packs."

"Those animals will have sand sores come the end of this." Hussein shrugged. "But sores can be cured. Remember that camels were built by Allah for the desert. In every way. They have nose flaps that close during sandstorms—their own kind of protection."

"Protection," Matthew thought aloud. "We ought to rouse ourselves enough to plan for our own protection come the end of this storm. We ought to be plotting an escape from Rakik and his band of blue giants. . . ."

Hussein shrugged a second time. "There is no point. We could leave the caravan at any time, but on foot . . ." He settled back into the sand. "On foot and without water, we would be pressing even Allah's mercy."

The silence within the tent resumed.

It was hard for any of them to goad themselves from the lethargy that had set in. The wind continued to howl, but they no longer heard the sand striking the tent. Matthew pushed himself upright. There must be huge drifts building outside, drifts bigger than from snow-storms in colder lands. He stared more carefully at the tent walls, then at the arch of the low ceil-ing. The tightly woven camel-hair threads let in little illumination. "You say it is morning now, Hussein?"

"You see me, do you not?" the guide listlessly replied.

"Barely. Why isn't there more light?"

Hussein pointed to the very center of the ceil-ing. "Because it comes only from there, *nasrani.*"

Matthew studied the dim glow of the oval. Something finally registered in his sluggish brain. "We're being buried alive!" he yelped. "That's why we have so little energy. We're using up our air supply! We've got to dig a vent!"

"Don't fuss, lad," Cornwall mumbled. "It will all be over by and by."

"By and by we'll all be dead!" Matthew forced himself onto his knees. "What happened to your collection of daggers, Hussein? I've got to cut a hole, then—"

"You don't want to let in more sand, Matthew Morrissey," the doctor fretted. "You don't want to go into that storm, either. It's not fit for man nor beast out there."

"And the Tuareg have taken my weapons," Hussein finished.

"Then I'll have to dig through from the flap," Matthew declared. And he set to the task with as much energy as he could muster.

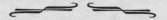

Sand dunes were unquestionably different from snowdrifts. Matthew yearned for the cold, clean, compact snow of a New York City winter. He longed for the chill purity of ice. What he struggled through instead was cascading, choking sand. It clung like molasses to every inch of his body, yet it was bone dry. Twice Hussein had to pull him by his legs back into the tent after he had been inundated by avalanches of sand. He crouched inside, hacking grains from his throat and lungs. But he didn't give up. On the third attempt, Matthew broke through.

"Hamdullah."

His thanks were short-lived. Above him a purple sun fought to cut through a mud-brown sky. Around him the sand still swirled in vicious eddies. The wind bowled him to his knees, and he grabbed for his turban cloth to wind around his nose and mouth. There was air, but it wasn't fit to breathe. He made a valiant attempt to search for the other tents, for the camels, but everything was masked by sand. Matthew stumbled backward, searching for his own tent. The few moments spent within the heart of the storm had so disoriented him that he nearly lost his way.

But yes, there it was. There was something else, too. Imbedded in the sand circling his tent were footprints. He bent and squinted through the cutting haze to inspect them. Not ordinary footprints, not his own. They were, instead, the tracks of a giant cat. Matthew blinked, and when he reopened his eyes the tracks had disappeared in a whirlwind. In a new frenzy, he attacked the piles of sand around the tent flap, realized he was making no headway in clearing an air vent, and finally managed to worm his way back inside the shelter.

"Well?" drawled Cornwall.

Matthew lay sprawled on the floor of sand, coughing. At last, words came out.

"Tell me more about the *jinn*, Hussein."

The guide raised an eyebrow in question, but when Matthew only lay there heaving for more breath, he finally spoke. "What is there you do not know already, *nasrani*? They favor ruins and cemeteries. They are shape-shifters, and travel in whirlwinds—"

97

"Are they always malevolent?" Matthew managed to wheeze out.

"The *ifrit*, the most powerful among the *jinn*, are known to take strong likes and dislikes. . . ."

"I thought as much."

Cornwall cleared his throat. "Superstitious nonsense. All of it. What's it got to do with this sandstorm? What's the verdict from your travels outside, lad?"

Matthew gave one more racking cough and sat up. "Outside? It's hopeless."

Hussein nodded, more than content to change the subject. "What will be will be."

Matthew was not at all happy with this Eastern brand of philosophy, but he had to admit to himself that for the moment he was stuck with both *jinn* and *kismet*.

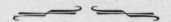

Precisely five days after the storm began, it ended. The wind just stopped. It took a while before Matthew and his tentmates actually noticed the hush, the absence of sound. Then Matthew burrowed again. He popped his head from the dune like a groundhog, to inspect a reborn world. The sky was crisp, the air was clean. The sand was where it belonged. He pulled himself upright and shook. Around him blue men were emerging from their own buried tents, doing the same thing. In his euphoria Matthew felt a sudden oneness with his fellow survivors. They were human, too. Then one of the Tuareg spied him.

"You!" His whip—already in hand—lashed out at Matthew. "Tend the camels!"

The days that followed the sandstorm should have been a joyous reintroduction to life. Instead, they were just like the days that had come before. The blue men were still in charge. Matthew and Dr. Cornwall and Hussein were still enslaved to them. Gin was the only one who had changed.

Matthew wasn't sure what had happened during the five days his dog had spent sequestered in a tent with Rakik, but some decision had obviously been made within his canine brain. The new Gin adamantly refused to ride atop any camel. The new Gin planted his paws firmly in the sand and bared his teeth at the sheik. Rakik finally gave up and allowed the dog to pad freely next to Ali again. Now he often trotted to the rear of the caravan to keep Matthew company, too. Matthew had little time to give to Gin, but in a few stolen moments at the end of each day, they communed.

"So," Matthew wrestled with Gin as in the old days. "You've remembered who you really belong to after all."

Gin writhed with pleasure and managed to lick his master's face.

"I knew you'd return to your senses one of these days." Matthew hugged the beast. Then he whispered in his ear. "But don't ignore that villain Rakik completely. Keep on his best side just until I figure how to get us out of his grasp for good."

Gin yipped agreement and Matthew shoved his rump. "Back to the sheik, now. Fawn on him. We all have our roles to play."

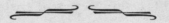

Matthew pondered his own role very hard over the next week. Now more accustomed to the backbreaking work of loading the animals, he sat atop his camel flexing his muscles when the work was finished for the morning and the caravan en route at last. There were new muscles to flex, muscles he'd never known he had. And with the fresh ease of his body, his mind felt sharp again, too. He began plotting extravagant schemes for freeing himself and his friends from Rakik's clutch. Nothing came of them, of course, until the day their route crossed that of another caravan working its way from the south.

The first glimpse of the caravan filled Matthew with excitement. It was not only the excitement of new faces, but the hope of potential liberation from the Tuareg. Surely someone within this new company would be civilized enough to see and understand the plight of Matthew and Dr. Cornwall and Hussein. It was a very long line of camels, after all. It drifted across the entire southern half of the horizon: hundreds of camels, perhaps as many as a thousand. As the string crept closer, though, Matthew noticed something odd. To the far side of the camels was another line. This one was black against the sand, and appeared to be shuffling along on foot. Coming ever nearer to each other, a curious new sound was added to the animal noises, the chanting of the drivers, the harness bells of the camels. Matthew cocked an ear to try and distinguish the sound. It was a kind of clanking, a grinding of metal upon metal—almost like . . .

Chains!

His body stiffened as the day's halt was called. But before he dismounted, he peered more closely across the distance. The walkers were staggering closer to the meeting point. The column as long as the camels was made up of Africans:

black Africans completely naked save for the heavy iron collars encircling their necks, and the shackles binding their ankles. As the sight fully registered, the horror of a practice he'd only partially fathomed washed over him. Matthew's ideas about right and wrong—good and evil— exploded. Sheik Ibn er-Rakik's caravan had rendezvoused with a true slaver.

Nausea overcame Matthew as his camel knelt. He stumbled off the animal and bent double over his racking stomach. What did he know of slavery until this moment? *Nothing.* The heaving began again as a new thought struck him. This could be the caravan Rakik had been seeking. The caravan to whom Matthew would be sold for his price in gold. Too soon, he himself could be added to that chained line of lost souls. Was there no solution to this terrible predicament?

The sharp slash of a whip across his shoulders was almost welcome. It brought Matthew back to his senses and cleared his mind admirably. *Work now. Change the world later.*

The meeting place was a hollow between dunes that held one of the Great Sand Sea's hidden wells. The well itself would have remained an absolutely innocuous hole in the sand if not for what surrounded it. As Matthew led the first of many camels to be watered, he stopped cold. Even the camel's thirst for the water couldn't move him. The well itself had no walls built of stone, but it did have a halo—a broad rim decorating its perimeters. This was made of *bones*: tens of thousands of weathered bones that had grown into an undulating hill. As his camel lunged vainly for the water trough, Matthew picked out a few camel carcasses in the pile. But the rest were human. He had the experience to know. Countless human skulls and bones had been piling up in this place over how many years?

Matthew was prodded from behind. "Move, *nasrani*. The beasts are thirsty."

"Hussein?" He spun. "How long have the slavers been coming to this well?"

"Many years. For centuries."

"This business has been going on for centuries?"

Hussein made a sharp motion of caution. "Water the camels and see nothing. Say nothing. Only pray to Allah that your own bones are not added to that pile."

CHAPTER NINE

THE NEW CARAVAN HAD COME OUT OF TIMBUKTU, AND its leaders were not Tuareg, but Arabs. When his work was finished, Matthew skulked around in the twilight before nightfall, trying to learn more about the caravan's intentions, its destination—and his own future. Rakik was meeting with the Arab captain, whose name even the Tuareg spoke with a combination of respect and apprehension: Muzzafir. The two leaders had been in conference for some time, seated on

104

cushions within Rakik's tent, its flaps propped open to catch the evening breeze. Matthew wished he could be a fly on the wall of that tent to eavesdrop on their conversation, but all he could catch were the sounds of tea being delivered by the Arab's servant, the clink of the teapot against tiny cups, and the low drone of the ritual opening of an official conversation.

Deciding he'd gain little from remaining near the two leaders, Matthew crept outside the boundaries of the camp to where the Africans were gathered. These people were silhouetted against the indigo sky, heaped in piles almost like the bones around the well. He approached them cautiously, wishing neither to alarm them, nor to call the Tuareg's attention to himself. Choosing a man who was less slumped than the others, Matthew slid down onto the sand before him.

"Salâm aleikoum," he tried. "Greetings."

Terrified stares surrounded him, except from the man he'd addressed. This one stretched his chained neck higher. "Good evening," he replied in halting Arabic. "What does the master desire?"

Matthew held up a hand. "I am no master. I am a slave, like you."

Disbelief crossed the man's face. "Where are your shackles? You walk free." The African turned away. "Do not play with me. My spirit has been grieved enough."

Matthew glanced over his shoulder. No one was watching. He inched closer. "The Tuareg— the blue men—captured my caravan. They murdered most of my comrades. They say they will sell me to your masters."

The story caught the man's attention. He turned back. "I have never seen a white slave. I thought only my people were taken into captivity."

"You are their leader?" Matthew guessed.

His shoulders straightened an inch. "In my country I am a chief." They slumped again. "Now my station is of little purpose."

"Here." Matthew reached beneath his robes and pulled out two locust balls. His dinner. He offered them. "I am Matthew. Matthew Morrissey. Perhaps we can help each other."

The African stared at the food for a long moment. At last he gravely accepted the gift. One lump went into his mouth, the other was given to a woman by his side. Matthew watched as she, in turn, divided the ball in two and fed half to a child in her lap before eating her share.

"Your wife?" he asked.

The man nodded. "And my son. There were two daughters once, but their bones are scattered on the sands."

Matthew sat back and bowed his head. "Your sorrow is my sorrow."

"Why should this be?" growled the black man. "He who has not walked in my steps cannot feel my pain."

Matthew raised his head and stared boldly into the angry brown eyes confronting him. "I have walked in your steps. I have felt your pain. My whole family is lost forever."

Some of the anger faded. "What do you want of me?"

Searching carefully for the right answer, Matthew finally said, "Your name, if you will share it."

Emaciated muscles tightened. "I am Yow Asanti Ay. From the green forests of the south."

"Thank you." Matthew rose. He'd pressed enough for tonight. "Tomorrow, at this same hour, I will bring more food. As much as I am able." He turned to go, then paused. He needed to say something else. What? Words came of their own volition:

"As you walk under the hot sun of the day, try to remember the road back to those green forests. One day soon you may be able to lead your people home."

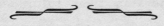

Matthew spent a restless night outside Cornwall's tent. He'd made a big promise—an impossible one—to the African chief. Not the food part. That was manageable, one way or another. What kept him tossing were those other words that had slipped off his tongue so easily; too easily. He'd suggested the possibility of life and liberty for Asanti and his people.

Now guilt racked him. He'd had a need to make Asanti feel better, but implying the potential of freedom? It was too much for Matthew to promise. Too much for anyone.

How had the Africans let themselves be enslaved to begin with? Why had they accepted this enslavement with such docility? He was a slave himself, yes, but the comparison ended with the word. How could Asanti and his people allow themselves to be so cruelly victimized? Matthew's anger grew before he recognized the truth: hunger, for one thing. Being marched naked in chains, for another. He shivered at the very thought of joining their misery, of being stripped and shackled.

Matthew fought past his nausea at the very concept of true slavery, of the way these human beings were being treated. Of the way he could be treated in the very near future. He began to think.

His first realization—which he was finally able to admit to himself—was that he and Dr. Cornwall and Hussein had no way out of their own dilemma without help. They were only three against too many. They needed manpower to overcome the Tuareg, and now the Arabs, too. As weak and sickly as these Africans were, there were so many more slaves than keepers. If they could only be roused and organized. . .

Matthew bolted upright. *We could help each other. We could become allies in an escape attempt.*

But how? He sank into his bed of sand again.

Cornwall's advice would be to use logic on the problem. Logically, Matthew needed to learn what would wake these people. He literally twisted himself into knots over the puzzle, bumping Hussein in the process. Hussein grunted and turned over on the sand. Matthew stared at the sleeping guide, curled up like Gin. . . . What made human beings different from animals? The ability to think, yes. And in thinking, to be able to strive, to aspire to something better in life . . .

Hope.

Hope was the most important thing needed. Didn't he himself need to keep the fires of hope burning? Didn't he need to keep alive the knowledge that someday there would be an end to his personal slavery, an end to the Great Sahara

Desert? For this, it was essential to keep his body strong. Therefore, or *ergo*, as the doctor would say, food was the next critical item. But without the hope, even more food wouldn't help.

Matthew suddenly realized that perhaps his words to the African had been the correct ones after all. They'd been the seed of a great idea. Now his job was to get some strength into Asanti and his family, into as many of the others as was humanly possible. . . . Strength of heart and strength of body. He had an idea about how to accomplish this. But he'd have to be very, very careful. Maybe the promise wasn't completely impossible. He just needed a miracle. But miracles, like *jinn*, had to be believed in before they could come to life. Faith—and a good plan— were all.

Satisfied for the moment, Matthew wound himself into a ball within his robes and slept at last.

Dawn was not Asa B. Cornwall's best moment.

"You want me to do *what*?" He rubbed his eyes and glared at Matthew. The doctor disliked being woken earlier than usual.

"I want you to tell Rakik that a big holy day is coming up. The most important day of the year in your faraway land. A day filled with signs and portents. Be convincing. You need to tell him that you wish to celebrate this festival of *magic* when we arrive at the next well."

"Why would I want to do anything like that?"

Matthew bent closer to Cornwall's ear. "Because you'd like to be free someday. Someday soon. Or had you planned on spending the rest of your life traipsing around the Sahara as Rakik's trained monkey?"

That got Cornwall out of his blankets. "Now look here, Matthew Morrissey, if you think for one moment that I enjoy my current position . . . if you think that Asa B. Cornwall, eminent phrenologist and author of some note, likes being kidnapped, so close to attaining another monumental victory, another pinnacle in his career—"

Matthew clapped a hand over the doctor's mouth. "We're right next to Rakik's tent. Lower your voice, sir. Please."

But Cornwall wasn't finished. He shook off the restraint. "We were so close to Siwa, Matthew. So close to the trail of Alexander the Great!" He flopped back onto his mat, tears of frustration in his eyes.

"I know, sir," Matthew soothed. "But Alexander isn't going anywhere. He'll wait for us. Try to collect yourself. I beg you!"

Cornwall snuffled. Matthew took that as permission to continue.

"Here's the situation. I need to get some food into the Africans—"

"Why you?"

"Because there's no one else! Most of them don't look as if they'll be able to last another day, much less walk all the way north to the Mediterranean for whatever's waiting for them there."

"Slave markets," Cornwall allowed. He rubbed at his nose and hoisted himself on an elbow. "In Tripoli. According to Hussein they'll be auctioned off, mostly to harems in Arabia. Which also means"—Cornwall gulped audibly—"the strongest males will be turned into eunuchs somewhere along the way. Usually at a place called Ghadames. Apparently there's a whole line of ancient fortresses hidden in the sands. First Zuila, then Ghadames, then—"

Matthew broke in. "What's a eunuch?" he asked suspiciously.

In the dim light of the tent Cornwall's face went pale. "You don't want to know, lad. But they end up protecting harem ladies, it seems."

"From what?"

"Umm," Cornwall hedged. He plucked at his nightshirt. "From unwanted male attention to the sultan's women."

"But putting men to guard women like that . . . isn't it sort of like letting a fox into the henhouse?"

Cornwall sighed. "After this little operation in Ghadames, they wouldn't be foxes anymore, lad."

Matthew sank back on his haunches. "Ouch."

"Precisely."

Sweat was rare in the desert, but Matthew was suddenly drenched with it. "Could they do it—this operation—to me, too?"

"Never fear, Matthew. Apparently the sultans prefer black Africans for the job."

"But still . . ."

Cornwall patted a few stray hairs across his bald pate. "You were saying, before the conversation took this unfortunate turn . . ." He raised his voice. "Something about a sudden need to feed the multitudes?"

"*Shhh. We need* them. They're part of my escape plan. But they won't be any use at all without some strength in them."

"Ah." Understanding began to penetrate Asa B. Cornwall's eyes.

"Yes, *ah*. The excuse for improving their rations—only temporarily, Rakik and the Arabs are to understand—is that you need them to perform for your mystical festival. A festival that will bring great good fortune to its celebrants.

Emphasize the *great good fortune*. You know how superstitious most of these men are. Give them some nonsense about how the stars require many, many, strong bodies. You should be able to elaborate from there." Matthew considered further. "Find out how far this Zuila is, too. Maybe that would be the best place for everything to happen, after all. Before we get too close to . . ." He paused, afraid even to utter the word. Then he braced himself and did it. "Too close to *Ghadames*. Somehow I suspect that after Ghadames, the game might be over."

"Zuila. All right. But what kind of performance?"

"It doesn't matter! I'll work something out with the Africans' leader, Asanti. Some kind of huge dance that will require their chains to be removed . . ."

"Better and better," Cornwall muttered. He began getting into the spirit of the conspiracy at last. "And at some point the dance turns into an attack against our mutual captors—"

"Keep that thought, sir." Matthew smiled. "So the Africans have got to be fed. For as many nights as there are till our next big stop. Zuila."

"Why don't you explain all this to Rakik yourself, Matthew?"

"I don't want him suspicious. He gives me

enough odd looks as it is. Hussein will have to do the translating. Just make it good."

"Hmmm. An evening something like the Fourth of July, but for magicians . . ."

"That's the idea, sir. Keep thinking." Matthew withdrew to attend to his camels.

Hussein was not happy with his role in the plot.

"What! You desire me to bring attention to myself, attention to the doctor before Rakik and this Muzzafir? In our position it is madness! Allah has blessed us thus far, but to do this thing would be pressing our luck beyond even Allah's help! The healthy slave, the living slave, is seen only when the master wishes him to be seen."

"And do you wish to spend the rest of *your* life in captivity?" Matthew asked. "And what about *Ghadames*?"

"I am too old and too ugly to be made into a eunuch! Allah be praised."

"Are you sure? Absolutely certain?"

Matthew watched the little grain of doubt planting itself within Hussein's brain. When a film of sweat broke across his forehead, he knew he'd won.

"Tell me again this thing you want me to do."

But even goaded by fear, Hussein couldn't seem
to arrange an interview for Cornwall with Rakik
that evening. Matthew was forced back on his
own resources once again. He'd promised food,
and he'd find some. Heaven knew the Africans
desperately needed it. From what he could tell,
they were served only one meal a day: the thin
gruel he'd watched being scooped into gourds
from huge cauldrons early that morning.

In the end, Matthew borrowed from his old
caravan's food supplies while the Tuareg were
eating. He could manage only a single sack hidden beneath his robes, but he filled that sack to
bursting with dates and dried camel meat. Then
he waited for nightfall to haul it outside the
camp. Asanti was waiting. He rose from a mound
of huddled bodies and motioned Matthew to the
far side, out of sight.

"You kept your promise. You came again."

Matthew unhooked the sack from his belt. "I
keep my promises to those who will keep theirs."

Asanti didn't answer. Instead he motioned
into the darkness. Several men cautiously
approached, grabbed the sack, and began to dis-
tribute its contents.

"It's not much," Matthew apologized, "but—"

"One date is life to the starving man. It brings
the sweetness of hope."

"Yes," Matthew agreed. "Hope is everything."
He crossed his legs on the sand and settled in for
a conference he prayed would be every bit as pro-
ductive as that between Rakik and Muzzafir.

CHAPTER TEN

"WHERE HAVE YOU BEEN, *nasrani*?"

Matthew collapsed onto the sand in front of Cornwall's tent. "You waited up for me? Why?"

Hussein propped himself against a tent pole and stared into the starry sky. "I was worried. This interest in the black slaves, it will bring trouble on our heads."

"I've just come from the Africans. No one saw me. . . . How much more trouble could we get into, anyway?"

Hussein raised a hand and began counting off fingers. "First, torture. You have not seen what these desert sheiks can do to a man when they feel playful. . . . Next, death . . . and then there's *Ghadames*." He stopped. "*Nasrani* wishes more?"

Matthew shook his head. "What I wish, Hussein, is that you would explain this slave business to me. I just can't understand it."

"But you have slavery in your own country, do you not? The Africans who are not marched north are shipped west, across the sea."

"I guess you're right, but I've never seen it. Never seen a slave before in my life. They don't have them in New York City, thank goodness. Only in the South." Matthew focused on the stars, too. "I don't think I could live in the South of my own country."

Hussein gave one of his shrugs. "It is hard to understand your passion over this subject. For our plight, yes. But for the blacks? Slavery of black Africans has been going on since before Roman times. Forever. The whole of North Africa runs on slavery. The slaves work in the oases, work in the salt mines. The Tuareg profit from this."

"And the Arabs," Matthew threw in.

"Yes, Arabs, too. Without the slaves and the salt they produce, there would be no caravans crossing the desert."

Matthew's eyes followed the trail of a plummeting star. "How can you Muslims be so religious, and treat people this way?"

"There must be correct behavior. The Koran itself says this." Hussein spread his hands. "Alms must be given, women must be protected, slaves must be allowed certain rights."

Matthew turned to Hussein. "Do you truly believe those starving, naked people outside of our camp are being given their rights?"

"Those people, they are in a masterless, in-between stage. When they have acquired true masters, they will also acquire the rights due them."

"You mean they're in limbo? What comes next? Hell?"

"*Nasrani, nasrani,*" Hussein sighed. "I did not make this world. I only live within it."

"Well, I live within it, too. And I say that tomorrow it's time for you and Cornwall to beard Rakik."

Matthew turned away from Hussein and the stars and deliberately closed his eyes. Someday he would learn enough to understand the workings of the traffic in slaves. He didn't believe that it just kept happening because it was a centuries-long tradition. Sure, tradition was part of it—economics, too. Everyone was making a little

Kathleen Karr

money along the way. But from his own small experience with business he knew that there was usually someone at the top. He needed to know who was at the top of this particular chain. Someone had to be giving orders to the Tuareg, to the Arabs like Muzzafir. Someone was making the decisions, sending the caravans across the Sahara. Someone was getting very rich from this trade in human misery.

Asa B. Cornwall ran a handkerchief over his very damp forehead. "He bought it! I can't believe that Rakik could be dim enough to have bought the entire scheme—lock, stock, and barrel!"

"And Muzzafir, too," Hussein added. "It is Muzzafir who must waste extra food on his slaves."

"I'm not sure he's wasting it," Matthew said. "You know the slaves will bring more if they don't look half dead. Muzzafir would have had to begin fattening them up soon anyway—"

"Of course," Dr. Cornwall commented. "Like livestock."

"Probably at Ghadames, the last oasis before Tripoli," Matthew continued. "He's only agreed to begin the process a little earlier. The idea of entertainment amuses him."

121

"It was the 'great good luck' that really brought him around, though," Cornwall added. "His piggy eyes bulged and he reached for an amulet tucked beneath his robes."

The Tuareg had been much laxer with them since the rendezvous, but still the three captives remained cautious. They were hiding behind a sand dune in the twilight, Matthew popping his head over the rim every few minutes to watch cauldrons being readied for the unexpected late meal for the Africans. He hadn't visited Asanti's camp this evening. It didn't seem necessary with another round of gruel in the offing. As yeasty smells began drifting their way, Matthew asked the obvious question. "How long is the journey to Zuila?"

"Only ten days, Allah be praised," Hussein replied. "A day or two more of extra food would have been too much to ask. All might have been lost."

"Too true," Cornwall added. "Once he let go of that amulet, Muzzafir was clicking over his abacus like a miser, working out supplies on hand versus distance to Tripoli. I strongly suspect that if our little revolt fails, the slaves will be placed on half their normal rations for the remainder of the trip anyway, traditional fattening in Ghadames or not. Muzzafir isn't a man to put more into his property than he can expect to get out of it."

"But if they fed these people better to begin with," Matthew fumed, "they'd end up with more of them surviving as far as the slave markets!"

"I don't think humane treatment is a concept Muzzafir could ever understand, lad." Cornwall patted Matthew's shoulder. "Probably has some cockeyed idea about the fittest surviving the ordeal."

Matthew edged his head over the dune a final time. "The guards are beginning to pass out the gourds. Asanti has his people lined up. They look like wraiths in the night . . . swaying weakly . . . with just their eyes glowing. . . ."

Cornwall tugged him back. "Don't go all melodramatic, Matthew Morrissey. We've done the best we can for the Africans. We've gotten them their extra rations. Now it's time to work out the details of our little evening of wonder and enchantment in Zuila."

Matthew shook the stark image from his head and lowered himself onto the sand. "Since you mention it, there are a few items I'll be needing." He began enumerating. "Shovels, paint, a coffin—"

"A coffin?" Cornwall burst out. "What in heaven's name do you intend to do with a coffin?"

"Well," Matthew admitted, "any elongated, body-sized box would do."

"But—"

"I've been spending a great deal of time thinking about Monsieur Robert-Houdin, Doctor."

"That elegant magician in the boulevard du Crime?"

"Exactly."

"Ah." Cornwall smiled a little smile of sudden enlightenment.

"What is this thing, this person you talk about?" Hussein inquired with some dubiousness.

"Get me what I need, Hussein," Matthew answered, "and you'll find out. The box, especially. Surely one of these Arabs in the new caravan is carrying a chest of some kind?"

Hussein shook his head. "This is not Cairo, where you can find anything you need in the souks. I think paint will be impossible. As for your box . . . mostly the caravan is carrying blocks of salt, and some ivory. But I will search."

"Oh, and one more thing," Matthew added. "I noticed that a few of the Arabs from Muzzafir's caravan are carrying guns—"

"Traded from your American slavers in West Africa," Hussein broke in darkly. "I have watched them play with these new toys. They cause much envy among the Tuareg. Soon the desert will be filled with even more violence."

"I don't like guns either, but that's not the point."

"What is?" asked Cornwall.

Matthew grinned. "Where there are guns, there must be gunpowder. I need you to liberate that, too. As much as the Arabs have."

Hussein groaned. "Too much. You want too much!"

"Only freedom," Matthew answered.

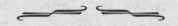

In the days that followed, Matthew met with Asanti each night after the extra meal had been served. A change began coming over the Africans. The extra food helped, of course, but now when Matthew arrived at the slaves' camp, there was a noticeable buzz circulating around the different groups. Asanti had set them to tasks suggested by Matthew, and the feeling of hope was strong in the air.

Matthew still arrived each evening with an extra sack of dates. As he emptied his own caravan's panniers of the food, he'd been carefully refilling the bags with sand so the theft wouldn't be noticed—at least for the moment. He didn't care to speculate on what might occur when the Tuareg finally went in search of dried dates—or the Arabs in search of gunpowder, or all the other little things Hussein was secretly collecting. With any luck, that wouldn't happen before

Zuila. And with more luck, they needn't worry about either the Tuareg or the Arabs after Zuila.

Asanti smiled each time he spied Matthew's food sack. The African chief always selected a few dates, then carefully allotted the remaining treats to his subleaders, and each night there were more men lined up for fruit and orders. To be absolutely certain of full cooperation on the Night of Nights in Zuila, Matthew finally explained the significance of Ghadames to Asanti. He watched the familiar sweat break out on the black man's brow.

"This is a true thing you tell me, Matthew?" Asanti asked. "We will be gelded like animals?"

"I swear it is true," Matthew replied. "Those who survive as far as Ghadames."

Asanti pounded a fist into his palm. "It would be better to die like a man in Zuila."

"I cannot lie, Asanti. Some of your people may die in Zuila. But if you stick together and don't lose your courage, more will live to be free."

Asanti reached for a date. "We become stronger each day. Our courage grows. We will not fail you."

Matthew cleared his throat. "About that other business. The magical box I told you about. Have you chosen the woman who will be my helper?"

Asanti raised his head. "My wife Afua will be the honored one."

Matthew gulped. "But I have explained to you some of the difficulties. I have been studying the swords carried by the masters, but there may be small differences in the curves . . ."

"It will be my wife."

Asanti had spoken. Matthew nodded acceptance and rose to leave. Now the pressure would be even greater. Robert-Houdin had used carefully measured, straight swords for his own onstage effects. Matthew prayed the rest of his memory was perfect on the subject of this particular trick of the great magician.

Five days passed, then six. After Matthew had Cornwall beg for an extra ration of water for the Africans during the middle of the day, when they usually stumbled through the scorching sun and heat dry-throated, chants began rising from the long line. It gave Matthew heart, and that night he asked Asanti what the singing had meant.

"They sing about home. They sing about slavery. They sing about the *razzia*, the manhunt." Asanti raised his head and cried out a few harsh-voiced lines. Then he translated:

"My sons are led from the abodes of men.
Salt and greed make them slaves."

When he sang again, his words sounded softer.

"At this hour,
Now,
'Round the fires our mothers sit.
Their hearts are filled with pain,
For we are stolen from the good green land.
But soon we shall return."

"Will you sing this at the dance in Zuila?" Matthew asked.

"This, and more," Asanti agreed. "The masters have not learned our language. They will not understand."

"Until it is too late," Matthew said.

Yow Asanti Ay smiled. "Until it is too late."

"I found your box, *nasrani*." Hussein sidled closer to Matthew as he unloaded a camel the next afternoon. He lowered his voice to a whisper. "It is filled with ostrich plumes. Very delicate."

Matthew straightened up from his task. "I'll need to work on it tonight. There are only three more days till we get to Zuila."

Hussein shook his head sorrowfully. "I don't see how—"

"You must talk to Rakik again. You and Cornwall. I'll need permission to work by a fire, officially and in the open. I'll be wanting light. I have a few tools in my own kit that should help."

"Always you need more," Hussein growled. "I find shovels, it is not enough. I see where the gunpowder lies hidden within kegs. The box, too—"

"The box is no good to us unless I fix it first, Hussein. You do want to be free of this lot, don't you?"

"It is easy for you," Hussein complained. "You don't have to stand before Rakik and Muzzafir with pictures in your mind. Pictures of bodies being flayed from the neck down, while the victims still breathe. Pictures of this skin being stuffed and used for balls—"

"Thank you for sharing that with me, Hussein. I'm sure it will improve my dreams tonight." Matthew stared the man down. Grumbling, Hussein set off on his odious errand.

Word of the coming Night of Nights had spread quickly through the caravan. Loading or unloading camels, sitting around evening fires, the men spoke of little else. As anticipation grew, it seemed there was nothing Rakik and Muzzafir were unwilling to contribute to the upcoming festivities in Zuila. As Matthew worked on the box between two fires that night, the Tuareg and the Arab sprawled on their cushions in close attendance to his every move. He tried to ignore their sharp interest, but it was hard.

Matthew had packed his own bag carefully back in Paris. He'd packed it anticipating a close encounter with the skull of Alexander the Great. Earlier encounters with the likes of Voltaire and Rousseau had suggested the usefulness of a crowbar. Since a crowbar was too heavy and unwieldy, he'd substituted a claw hammer and chisel. Always handy for the odd recalcitrant sarcophagus. As he squinted through the poor light for the marks he'd etched into the wood earlier, he wished he'd thought to pack a small file and saw as well. He made a mental note to add them to his kit for Cornwall's next expedition, then snorted ruefully to himself. If this batch of tricks didn't work, there'd be no next expedition. Matthew aimed the chisel, picked up the hammer and began to delicately carve out the first of the many slim, crescent-shaped holes that were necessary if Robert-Houdin's trick were to succeed.

Tap, tap, tap.

Rakik bent closer. "What is this you do, slave?"

Matthew kept tapping. He had only two more nights to finish the job, after all. "In Zuila, O Great Sheik, I will be the Master of Revels for Dr. Asa B. Cornwall. I help to prepare one of his most marvelous wonders."

"Explain it to me!" Rakik demanded.

"I am sorry, magnificent one, but that is impossible. The magic must be kept secret until the moment of its use during the Night of Nights."

Matthew imagined the petulant scowl now being hidden by the Tuareg's veil. "There will be other wonders as well, splendid captain of warriors and camels," he added. "Such as you have never seen, and will never see again in your lifetime."

He heard Rakik settle back on his cushion, mollified for the moment.

Tap, tap, tap.

"What have you done with my ostrich feathers?"

Matthew spun his head. Muzzafir's voice was high-pitched and whiny. It came from an obese, pampered body. Somehow the man, settled within his folds of fat, was scarier than Rakik. Matthew nodded deferentially.

"The feathers are safe, respected leader. They will travel in this same box until Zuila, and thereafter as well."

"Dust will enter the holes and damage the goods!"

"I will line the box with cloth to prevent that, esteemed master."

Muzzafir glared. "The feathers are worth *your* weight in gold, slave. You will pay—personally— for their ruin." The Arab suddenly giggled with pleasure, obviously visualizing one of Hussein's scenarios of torture.

"Of course, benevolent one."

Matthew turned back to the box. In his eyes it suddenly became a coffin again—quite an attractive one, if you imagined Muzzafir reposing in layers within it. He steadied his shaking hands and got on with the job.

CHAPTER ELEVEN

Matthew was totally dumbfounded when his camel topped a dune about midmorning the next day.

"Where's the sand?"

His yelp of surprise must have been loud, because the Tuareg riding in front of him condescended to answer for once.

"It is the end of the *erg* for now, slave. The Black Stone Desert begins."

It was well named. Matthew squinted into the

horizon at nothing but desolation. No life. A wasteland of flat, cracked, blackened earth and stone cooking under the unrelenting sun. He turned to the golden sand behind him that he'd believed would continue forever. Suddenly it seemed warm and hospitable, alive in its undulating waves. Too late. The caravan slid down the last dune and toiled forward.

By the time a campsite had been selected for the night, Matthew was worried about more than the landscape. He'd had to find Gin's boots and protect the dog's delicate paws once more, but there was no protection he could give Asanti and his people for their bare feet.

"This Black Stone Desert," he asked Hussein at the first opportunity, "how long does it last?"

"I've traveled this way once before in my youth, *nasrani*. It continues all the way to Zuila."

"For two more days, then?"

"Even so."

Matthew began praying for Asanti's people—and his great escape plans, too.

Zuila was a bizarre oasis set within a world of blackness. Their long caravan pushed hard to reach it by nightfall of the tenth day. When the setting sun glinted from the walls rising out of the desert, Matthew was certain he was seeing a mirage.

"Castles," he whispered. "Castles and towers within a fortress. In the middle of such a place?"

But it was real, as real as such a fantasy could be in the ever-changing Sahara. The camels stumbled through arches of tumbling stone, nose rings taut as they strove for the water they could smell within. And that was all the stone walls surrounded: a crumbling castle and several wells hacked out of the hardened earth. There were no palm trees, no groves of figs or dates, not a single sprig of grass within the ancient ruins. There were no people, either. There were, however, lizards—and scorpions to spare. Matthew trod on one of the huge insects just after he'd pulled on sandals and swung off his camel. He cringed at the squish. Around him, the Tuareg were stomping with energy. Matthew tore his eyes from the ground to see Hussein making his way toward him. The guide came to a stop.

"Cornwall has informed Rakik that the stars are not in the correct alignment for festivities tonight. He claims they will not be so until tomorrow. Allah be praised, the masters already planned to rest and water the animals for a full day."

"You mean I have all of tomorrow to finish preparations?"

Another colossal scorpion scuttled by and Hussein efficiently dispatched it. Then he nodded. "As Master of Revels, you are to be excused from other labors tomorrow."

"Rakik would allow this?"

"Rakik and Muzzafir are both as consumed with curiosity as their men. They would do nothing to keep you from performing this role you have assumed."

"*Hamdullah!*"

"Save your thanks till after we survive this scourge of vermin, *nasrani*." Hussein studied the six-inch bug he'd just flattened. "They have grown since my last visit." He glanced at the surrounding walls as shadows fell with heavy finality. "Zuila has always been a place of mystery, never of comfort."

Hussein decamped, leaving Matthew grasping his mount's reins, staring at the closest well. The Africans were shoving camels aside as they fought for spots at the watering troughs. The successful slaves were on their knees, heads lowered, lapping water like the animals. The exposed heels of feet protruding from ankle shackles were as cracked as the Black Stone Desert, only these cracks bled red. Would these people be able to dance tomorrow night? Would they be in any condition to fight for their lives?

Zuila was turning out to be vastly different from Matthew's dreams of it. He shook his head and went in search of a vat of sheep fat. Asanti would be needing it.

Cornwall was up late into the night tending to a spate of scorpion-sting victims. Matthew worked beside the doctor, learning how to draw venom from the wounds, then helping to prepare poultices to further the healing. Scorpions were apparently both color- and caste-blind. They struck equally at Tuareg, Arab, and slave. By midnight, when the crisis had slowed for the moment, there were more than a dozen of the stricken lined up on mats outside the castle.

The doctor finally straightened from his labors. "Funny how the thrill of proving ancient medical procedures correct can pall in the light of an epidemic. All one's left with is hard work and perspiration." He studied the victims. "There's little more we can do for these poor souls, Matthew. Morning will tell us where we've succeeded . . ." He sighed. "Or failed."

The sliver of a new moon, a crescent moon, hovered above them. In the light from it and the stars Matthew had the chance to really inspect the place for the first time since the crisis began.

"Where are we, sir?" He pointed at the ramparts, then the towers. "What is this strange place all about?"

Cornwall rubbed his forehead. It glistened with beads of sweat, and he looked worn out. "From the studies I did back in Paris, it seems that the Romans built a string of forts to defend their desert domain from the wild tribes of their time." He shook his head. "But this is not Roman, Matthew. The architecture is all wrong. The ramparts . . . and that dome on the building attached to the castle walls—it must be a chapel—they seem almost Byzantine."

"Byzantine?" Matthew asked.

"The empire that took over after the Romans fell," Cornwall explained. "It was based in Constantinople. I don't know . . ." Cornwall paused again. "But in my readings I did come across reference to a lost kingdom called Ceballa. It was reputed to be hidden deep in the desert of North Africa. It was also said to contain treasures beyond all understanding." Cornwall swiped at his head again. "Curious how fabled treasures mean so little next to life and death."

He tucked a blanket borrowed from his own tent around one of the bloated, moaning Africans, then gave the trembling hand of an Arab a reassuring squeeze. "I must get some rest.

You too, lad. We'll see what we can learn of this place in the light of a new dawn." He stopped, as if remembering. "Big day tomorrow. We've got to be ready for it." Cornwall turned to leave.

"Wait, sir," Matthew called. "Let me check your tent before you lie down. For scorpions."

Asa B. Cornwall smiled grimly. "It wouldn't do for the healer to be stricken, would it?"

Matthew led the way, with Cornwall following, muttering to himself. "Alexander never had to personally deal with any of this. Six-inch scorpions. Eight-inch scorpions. What're a few soldiers more or less when you've got thirty thousand at your beck and call? All he had to do was conquer the world."

After he'd assured the doctor's safety, Matthew found only troubled sleep for himself. He dozed for a while on the rock-hard ground next to Hussein, strange images floating through his head. There were man-sized scorpions, and lizards as big as houses. They appeared to be in competition with each other. The scorpions marched like worker ants with boulders of black stone in their pincers, making their way toward a giant fortress in the distance. The lizards roughly shouldered the stones from the insects, then

nosed them closer to the fortress. Atop the
fortress itself stood a single man, waiting. In his
dream, Matthew seemed to be flying over the two
armies, closer and closer to the man. He was a
stonemason, and he calmly accepted the rocks,
professionally chipped them into neat squares
with a few blows from his hammer and chisel,
then laid them upon each other, mortaring the
seams, building the fort ever larger. When the
man looked up, Matthew saw his face. With a start
he jerked awake, drenched in sweat.

It was his father.

Sleep gone, Matthew rose as if being sum-
moned. The crescent moon was much lower in
the sky. The night had turned cold. He tightened
his robes and set off through the slumbering
camp for the ramparts that were calling to him.

Matthew fumbled along the inner walls till he
came to a circular tower filled with spiral stone
steps that should take him to the top. Inside, it was
pitch-dark. He groped out blindly for the rounded
wall, then mounted the worn steps, revolution by
revolution. He began to feel as if the tower were
leaning in toward him; began to feel that there *was*
no top, no outlet. And then he broke through.
The ramparts stretched to either side of him,

solid dark lengths that outlined the desert beyond and the stars above. He leaned against the nearest parapet wall, taking in the extraordinary, alien beauty of the spot. On such a night, in such a place, anything was possible. . . .

A faint scraping against nearby stone made Matthew spin.

"No!"

It couldn't be, yet it was. Again. It was close, perched on a broken section of wall not five yards away.

"My cheetah," he whispered.

The cat stared at him with eyes that glinted like molten amber through the darkness. Matthew stared back, mesmerized for long moments. Then the creature casually broke the connection, raised a powerful paw, and delicately began licking it. Matthew remained terrified; too petrified to move. Yet there was a certain fascination. . . . Did he really want to move?

"My *jinn*," he murmured. "My personal *jinn*. Do you bring me luck—or something else?"

Its grooming complete, the cat spared him another glance, and sprang—but not at Matthew. Instead it gracefully glided to the top of the tower, then disappeared into the night.

"Hamdullah," Matthew prayed. "Thank you, God. Once more."

"Give praise where praise be due, and all good things will come to you."

Matthew spun again, this time in the opposite direction, toward the singsong voice. It was an old voice, cracked and rusty, as if it hadn't had much practice for many years, for centuries. The figure Matthew spied was bent and robed, its head cowled within folds of cotton black as the night.

"Who—who are you?" he stammered.

"Father Moses, that be me. Zuila is my watch to see."

"But I don't understand—"

A cackling laughter was his response, until the figure moved closer and grasped out for Matthew's arm with skeletal fingers that had a leathery, scaled sheen—as if the old man had been dining on lizards for eons. Maybe he had. He spoke again, pulling Matthew's eyes from those fingers.

"Young of mind and pure of heart, *you* shall have the victor's part."

"But, but—"

Protests were useless. Matthew was dragged in the viselike grip along the ramparts to the next tower. This he was pulled into and down, down, down. Certainly farther down than he'd ever climbed to reach the sky. Farther still they descended, the constant cackling of the ancient man the only sound penetrating the darkness, aside from the scuffle of their sandals. And farther yet they went, till surely they were beneath the ramparts, beneath the very desert itself.

The apparition stopped. Matthew's arm was released. He waited in total darkness till he heard the sound of flint scraping iron. A spark appeared and was nursed into flame. A candle was lit—but not one alone. The old man hobbled gleefully around the emerging room, lighting torches and candles, one after the other, until a brilliance Matthew had never conceived overwhelmed him.

He blinked, then rubbed his eyes and blinked again. The brilliance was coming from more than the sudden light. It was coming from piles of gleaming objects heaped about the close stone-walled chamber.

"I don't understand," Matthew said. "Gold?"

The cackle returned. "All these years I've kept it true—now the job must turn to you."

Matthew gaped at the madman. For surely he must be that. Yet gold there was. He knew the look of gold. He'd seen it in quantity before, thanks to Nicholas Mordecai. But that was lifetimes ago, in Philadelphia . . . and even Nicholas Mordecai had never amassed such a fortune.

Matthew bent to reach for a coin from among heaped thousands. He fingered the unknown face that was stamped upon it. "Who is this?" he tried once more.

"Justinian." The rhyming disappeared with the significance of the name. "Emperor of the World!"

"But that was—" How long ago? Dr. Cornwall would know. Matthew turned to the shining mounds of plates, goblets, urns, and jewelry, all refracting light from each other. His survey was halted by a partially hidden image on the floor beneath the treasure. Drawn to it, he knelt to clear the space. It was a picture, made from gleaming pieces of colored glass. It showed a mighty cat, *his* cat, springing . . .

Matthew swayed dizzily into the image and knew no more.

The pinks of breaking dawn woke Matthew. He stretched, then hoisted himself partially up. Where was he? Atop the ramparts? How had he gotten here? What was he doing here? He rubbed at his eyes. And what a strange dream he'd had. The whole night had been filled with strange dreams. He rubbed some more, then opened a tightly clenched fist. Something dropped from his hand to roll across the rough stone. It spun, teetered, and fell. Matthew struggled to his knees and reached for it. The sun rose another degree in the sky and cast a ray upon the object.

It seemed to be a newly minted golden coin.

Matthew flipped the coin to study a bearded face gracing the obverse side.

"Justinian. Emperor of the World!"

As the words echoed through his mind, Matthew staggered against the rampart wall. Justinian . . . the golden treasure trove . . . Father Moses . . . the cheetah. They'd been real. It had happened . . . and maybe his own father had been the guide to everything. He stared up into the sky.

"What does it all mean? Please tell me!"

He begged uselessly for an answer. The sun only rose another notch above the Black Stone Desert and the ramparts of Zuila.

Chapter Twelve

Matthew found Cornwall in front of the castle with his patients. He was looking pleased with himself.

"Where have you been, lad? Look here, they've all survived! Every last one of our scorpion victims is going to make it! It's a miracle!"

Matthew smiled as he caught his breath from his mad dash down from the ramparts. "No, sir. It's your care. Maybe you missed your true calling."

Hands were reaching out for Cornwall. When

he bent to grasp them, his fingers were smothered with grateful kisses. He blushed. "Medicine? Who knows, Matthew? Life takes strange detours."

"It certainly does, sir."

Cornwall turned to a few loitering Arabs. "Get the patients under cover for the day. Somewhere cool. And keep a guard posted to kill any lurking scorpions!" When blank faces were his only response, the doctor tugged at his robes in frustration. "The language barrier, I keep forgetting. Explain to them, Matthew."

Matthew explained, directed the evacuation of the patients, then had Cornwall to himself at last. Seeing the stricken laid out before the doctor had brought him back to reality once more. It had also made him begin to doubt his recent experiences all over again. "I need to speak to you about something, sir. Something curious, but possibly important."

Asa B. Cornwall swiped at his brow. "Drat, I'm sweating again. I shouldn't be sweating in this dryness. . . . Is it about tonight? Because I think, possibly, that I might have to rest during the heat of the day myself."

Matthew pulled out the golden coin. "I'm not certain what it's about, but you need to have a look at this."

Cornwall looked. "Justinian the First? He was a sixth-century emperor of the Byzantine Empire. Where in the world did you find this?"

Matthew reached to cover the coin in the doctor's outstretched palm as several Tuareg came into view. "Privately. Let's talk privately, please."

Asa B. Cornwall shook his head. "I'd certainly like to see that mosaic you described, lad. Not to mention the other trinkets. But as for the rest—"

Matthew had recounted everything in the privacy of the doctor's tent. Everything except the encounter with his own personal *jinn*. If Father Moses was hard to accept, that cheetah would be impossible.

"—I don't know, Matthew. I'm having a little trouble thinking clearly."

The doctor was sweating again. And occasional shudders had begun running through his body.

"Are you getting sick, sir?" Matthew asked. He wanted to add *Sick today, of all days?* but couldn't. It wouldn't be fair.

"Strange symptoms," murmured Cornwall. "Slight dizziness, the odd tremor, probably a fever . . ." He stretched out flat on his mat. "The only thing I can think of is malaria. Remember all those mosquitoes a while back? My studies in

Paris suggested an incubation period of four weeks. . . . I'm truly sorry. Miserable timing."

Matthew was already rooting through Cornwall's medicine case. He pulled out a bottle. "Quinine. I knew there was a reason we've been lugging it around for so long. We've got to get some quinine into you right now!"

"I hadn't even thought that far—"

Matthew offered a strong dose. "Take this and rest, sir. You've only got to be in good enough shape to put in an appearance tonight. I'll take care of the rest."

The doctor swallowed, not even complaining about the vileness of the taste. "Bless you, lad. I have complete faith in you." His eyes glazed over as his head sank back once more. "Just . . . try to take a minute to check our patients?"

"Don't worry yourself, sir. I will. I'll take care of everything."

Matthew gently unwound Cornwall's turban, then used the cloth to swab at the doctor's dripping face. Finally he sank back on his heels to think. Malaria surely seemed to pick its moments. What could he do? Where to start on everything else? The rock-hard dirt beneath him gave him his hint. *Shovels.* He'd start with the shovels and Asanti's people. Judging by the density of this ground, it was going to take all day for the

Africans to dig a hole big enough for his opening trick.

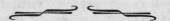

Matthew had been spinning around like a dervish all morning, setting up props for the evening. He felt as if he were constructing a tower out of cards. One false move and it would all come toppling down, dashing his hopes for freedom—dashing the Africans' chance at life. His big break came at noon. He'd set Hussein to watch over the trench Asanti's men were digging behind a hastily erected screen of tent cloth.

"Nasrani—" Hussein found Matthew checking on the scorpion victims. *"Nasrani,"* he whispered in his ear, "you had better come at once."

Matthew finished changing a poultice on the leg of a particularly large Tuareg. "What is it?"

Hussein tugged. "Come."

They left the cool, protective rooms of the castle for the solid, living heat of the outer courtyard beneath the fortress walls. This is where the festivities would be held. Hussein led Matthew to the far corner tower, well away from the huddled tents and resting camels. It was the area Matthew had selected as his stage, and it was where the Africans were still digging. Hussein pulled Matthew behind the screen.

"Look!"

Matthew whistled long and low. "What luck!"

Asanti joined them, tall and proud. He was tall and proud because Matthew's first major task of the morning had been to convince Muzzafir to remove the neck and ankle shackles of Asanti and all the men who would be helping him today. It hadn't been easy. Matthew could almost see himself being flayed in the villain's mind before assent was given.

"See what we have found, Matthew." Asanti smiled. "Is it a help to you?"

"I'll say!" He whistled again. At the bottom of the pit the diggers had discovered the roof of an underground tunnel. Strategies for its potential use nearly overwhelmed him, but Matthew shook them off. There was no time to waste on fantasies. First he needed to know where this tunnel went. He jumped into the pit and eased his body through the gap that had been broken through the stone arch of the roof. It was too much to hope for, but he prayed anyway. *"Please let it lead beyond the fortress walls. Let it open into the desert. Please—"*

When his sandals touched ground, he paused only long enough to get his bearings, then scurried through the darkness toward a dim illumination beyond. When he pulled himself up into the daylight once more, he found himself behind a boulder, thirty yards from the fortress walls. Matthew gave a leap of joy, came down hard on an enormous scorpion, and returned through the tunnel with considerably more care. Hussein was waiting to pull him out.

"What did you find, *nasrani*?"

"A miracle." He beamed. "A true, genuine, verifiable miracle! Thank you, Lord. *Hamdullah!*" He bowed his head in thanksgiving for a moment, then turned to Asanti and business.

"Get more men on the job. Clear away the tunnel roof completely. Build a ramp going down into it that a camel can descend upon. I'm certain the tunnel's high enough. . . ." His brain was operating faster than the words could spill out. "Make sure the opening outside the walls is big enough for a camel, too. And make sure none of the masters sees any of this!"

Asanti nodded his head. "For you we will accomplish all of this before nightfall. For you we will do anything."

Hussein stood frowning to one side. "I don't understand these orders you give, *nasrani*."

Matthew clapped him on the shoulder. "Hussein, tonight you are going to see one of the great Robert-Houdin's tricks performed as never before."

Hussein was unconvinced. "What is this trick?"

Matthew smiled broadly. "I'm renaming it, Hussein. I'm calling it *The Mystery of the Disappearing Camel.*"

━━━━━━ ━━━━━━

The afternoon continued far better than Matthew could have hoped. This was mainly because the Arabs and Tuareg were taking their day of rest seriously. A few of them had appeared for midday prayers, but through the blistering heat of the afternoon they all slunk back into their tents for long, comfortable naps. Matthew, Hussein, and the Africans worked straight through. With the wells nearby, they could stop for drinks or to douse themselves with refreshing water as often as they liked, and Asanti's men worked with a will. When Matthew was fairly certain that the tunnel was going to be usable, he sat down with Asanti and laid out his revised master plan. Asanti's eyes grew wider and wider as he digested all of the ramifications.

"How did you come by this wisdom, Matthew? It is beyond your years. Beyond the years of most men."

Matthew shrugged. "I'm not wise, Asanti. Only desperate. And we could still fail—"

"No!" The chief's dark eyes hardened. "Do not speak of failure. It will happen as you say."

Matthew excused himself to finish the remainder of his preparations. Who knew how the night would play itself out? The best-laid plans . . .

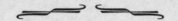

All the dirt from the pit had to go somewhere. Matthew decided that rather than trying to hide it, he'd use it. The sun was beginning to set, and the day to cool, when he stood back to admire the small ceremonial mound he'd had Asanti's men create. They'd set some of the stones from the roof of the tunnel into the side of the hill as steps, and several other stones held up a flat slab of rock on the top. Matthew was pleased. It looked like an altar to some ancient god. It would also make a terrific bench for the ailing Dr. Cornwall to rest upon between his necessary parts in the performance.

"I wish to know something, slave."

Matthew started. It was Muzzafir, dressed in fresh robes and looking pink and rested. The villain had waddled up to him with amazing stealth. "Your wish is my command, master."

"Naturally. But what I wish to know is how you—a mere stripling, a cursed infidel slave—how you have caused these blacks to work so hard today."

"Even black slaves may look forward to festivities, master." He paused. Muzzafir was really more than just a little naturally pink. And there was a certain unmistakable odor emanating from the man. Something Matthew hadn't smelled in a very long time. "It helped that you were gracious enough to relieve them of their chains for the work."

"They will be returned soon enough."

"Of course, master." Was it possible? It had to be. The man had been drinking *alcohol*. Matthew decided to take a chance. "But in the meantime, would the worthy master extend his benefactions to the dancers who are to perform tonight?"

Muzzafir frowned with petulance. "Cannot any black dance? Let those already without shackles do the work."

Matthew knew Muzzafir couldn't tell one African from another. "Those who labored for me today and will continue to labor for me throughout the festivities are not dancers. The chosen dancers are others—others quite expert who will thrill you with their performance."

Muzzafir growled, staggered slightly, but reached for the iron key hanging from his belt. "Here!" He tossed it to Matthew. "Remove the chains yourself. I have better things to do. But if a single one of my slaves escapes—"

"Where would they escape to, O most kind and considerate master? Do you see anything but death outside this fortress for any soul on foot without food and water?"

"True," Muzzafir reluctantly agreed. "In the Sahara chains enslave the mind, not the body."

Matthew bowed his thanks. Even intoxicated, Muzzafir might be more intelligent than he let on. He'd need to be watched.

As Muzzafir lurched away, Hussein appeared. Matthew tossed him the key.

"By Allah's beard! How did you come by this?"

"Our master is two sheets to the wind."

"I do not know these words, *nasrani*."

"I thought Muslims did not drink alcohol, Hussein, but Muzzafir—"

Hussein shrugged understanding. "Hidden bottles have been found and opened behind tent flaps all afternoon. It can happen after long months in the desert. There are some unwilling to await the delights of the Gardens of Paradise."

"Others have been drinking as well?"

Hussein nodded, a little embarrassed by the admission. "Many."

"Allah is good indeed, my friend." Matthew grinned. "Get to work with that key, Hussein. Our captors are welcome to totter, but I believe that *all* of Asanti's people should walk tall and proud this Night of Nights."

CHAPTER THIRTEEN

THE CRESCENT MOON HAD GROWN. AS IF REFLECTING the flames below, it shone with a strange reddish hue. Matthew stood atop his ceremonial mound directly beneath the tower and ramparts of the fortress—and this bloody moon. The matching crescent scar on his cheek was boldly outlined by the light of the halo of fires blazing around the mound. He stared for a long moment at the multitude seated before him. Rakik and Muzzafir were settled on opposite sides of the central aisle he'd marked out leading to the dancing circle just below the mound. The blue men were in a block radiating out from Rakik. The Arabs surrounded and spread away from Muzzafir. To the rear were the Africans, bearing unlocked chains that could be cast aside in a moment. They were so silent—their ebony nakedness blending so well with the night—that one could easily forget their presence. This was as it should be. Matthew needed them to remain as unobtrusive as possible until their moment arrived. His survey complete, he spread his robed arms wide.

"I, Matthew Morrissey, son of John, grandson of Seamus, born in the distant, fabled land of America, walker in the golden streets of New York, voyager on the seven seas; I, who have burrowed in the depths after mysteries beyond your ken, who have made offerings to the Almighty on the boulevards of Paris, who have cast the very face of evil itself from the cliffs of the lost island of St. Helena and have now become a wanderer of the Great Sahara—"

He paused to be certain he was weaving the proper storytelling web. Heads were bent forward in interest. He continued.

"I, Matthew Morrissey, young in years but rich in experience, present to you one who has journeyed vastly beyond any of my meager adventures. I present one who understands not only the hidden secrets of the earth, not only the inner mysteries of men's hearts and minds, but also the riddle of the stars. On this Night of Nights, this Festival of Festivals, I present to you the man who will lead us into new realms of wonder, fear, and delight."

Matthew bent to reach for the torch he'd prepared. It was his first signal to Asanti. A single drum sounded.

Tom. Tom. Tom.

The beat began slowly. Matthew lit the torch, flung it high into the heavens, caught it, brought it to his mouth, then spewed forth a stream of fire toward the trickle of gunpowder he'd carefully spread at the foot of the mound.

The drum increased its pace and volume.

TOM-tom-tom, TOM-tom-tom, TOM-tom-tom.

Catch, he prayed to himself. *Catch!*

The flame caught. A thin, bright trail of fire sped down the central aisle of the courtyard to end in a circle around the waiting figure of the doctor. He was swaying, his face preternaturally bright. It was the malaria.

Walk, Matthew silently urged. *Walk!*

The first drum was joined by a second.

TOM-TOM-tom, TOM-TOM-tom, TOM-TOM-tom...

Cornwall caught the rhythm and began careening toward the mound.

"I give you Dr. Asa B. Cornwall!" Matthew exulted.

The last of the flames flickered at the tail of his robes as Cornwall staggered to the foot of the mound. Matthew reached out a hand to grasp the doctor's and pulled him halfway to the top as the drums reached their crescendo and stopped. Cornwall steadied himself and turned toward the crowd, then Matthew. He blinked.

"I'm not going to make it through the night's events, lad. . . . Malaria is worse than I estimated. Far worse. I just cannot—" He crumpled into Matthew's arms.

Matthew swallowed hard as he faced the audience. *Improvise.* That's what he had to do. Fast. He raised his head high over Cornwall's body.

"The power of the stars is so strong this Night of Nights that the great Dr. Cornwall finds it necessary to withdraw into himself in silent meditation to focus the power—all the power of the universe—over Zuila. He will continue his meditations from the altar of Justinian!"

Matthew mounted the final step as if it were all part of the ritual and laid Cornwall's quaking body on the flat slab of stone. He arranged the arms and legs in a suitable pose, then bent to whisper in his friend's ear. "Don't worry, sir. Rest. Get well." But Cornwall's eyes were already out of focus. Matthew turned away.

"He begins his inner trip to the transcendent stars. Soon the great Asa B. Cornwall will be gazing down on us from the moon itself! Thence from Venus, from Mars, from Saturn and Jupiter—and even farther than the moon and planets, to the very edges of the universe." *But not too far, sir*, Matthew added in his mind. *Don't go so far that you can't return to me.* Matthew raised his arms once more, and stretched his head back to gaze at the moon. A rare night bird flew across its narrow face. The audience gasped.

"An omen!" someone cried out. He was joined by others shouting, "An omen! An omen!"

Matthew riveted his gaze upon the people. "You yourselves have seen the sign! It is as I said. Under the watchful eye and soul of Asa B. Cornwall, we will begin!"

"We will begin" was Asanti's next cue. The first drum started up again, with a different rhythm. Matthew descended the steps from the altar, relit his torch, and directed it toward the tower corner to his right. All signs of digging had been hidden by a tarp spread tightly over the ground of the courtyard.

"Behold the Stage of Illusions upon which our

revels will begin. For your amusement and pleasure, great Sheik Rakik, mighty master Muzzafir,
for the amusement and pleasure of the men who
bravely follow you into the depths of the Sahara,
a special magical trick has been devised. It is
called *The Mystery of the Disappearing Camel!*"

Matthew decorously progressed to the tarp.
"Merely observe the complete solidity of the
stage." He paced across it carefully, hoping his
footsteps would not vibrate and give away the
gaping hole beneath. He made it across, then
planted himself in front and to one side of the
fraudulent surface. He nodded to Rakik. "With
your permission, Sheik Ibn er-Rakik, I will make
one of your camels disappear into thin air from
this stage."

Rakik's eyes glinted above his veil. "Such a
thing is impossible."

Matthew stared back. "Nothing is impossible
on this Night of Nights, great Sheik."

Rakik nodded. "I give my permission. I wish to
see your wonder performed."

Matthew waved his torch like a conductor's
baton. "First we must build the Walls of Magic!"

Several of Asanti's men appeared from the
shadows, carrying more stretched tarps made
from tent poles and cloth. They carefully posi-
tioned these walls upright, behind and to

Matthew's side, almost completely boxing in the area of the covered hole. Matthew feigned disinterest in the proceedings, staring instead beyond the assembly.

"Bring on the camel!" he ordered.

All heads stretched back to watch as a fully loaded camel was led forward out of the darkness by an African. The animal complained vehemently at the injustice of being forced to work during the night. Arab and Tuareg alike chuckled as the camel's neck swung out and its teeth chomped blindly at the nearest humans. Under the cover of this entertainment, preparations were completed behind the false walls. When the camel was halted at the edge of the courtyard stage, two walls had turned into a covered hut with a side entrance. Matthew waved his torch again.

"Enter, O great ship of the desert. Enter into the magical tent! Allah go with you, for who knows what lies beyond?"

He waved once more and the drumbeats, which had become a part of the night, increased in fury as a third, a fourth, then a dozen drums joined in the cacophony. Matthew raised his arms, watching the camel lunge for the bait being offered from within—irresistible bait: a ball of honey-coated grain. As the camel's tail disappeared, he waited for the safe signal from Asanti behind the stage. It came. He brought his arms down, and the drums gave a final crash and were silent. Matthew wheeled back to his audience.

"Now you will observe, great Sheik, a true mystery of the Sahara before your very eyes." He motioned to Asanti's hidden men, and the front wall of the hut was slid open. "Seeing is believing."

A great sigh swept over the audience. Matthew exhaled a great sigh himself. The camel was well and truly gone. All that remained within view was the foreshortened rear wall of the hut. The trick had worked!

"Do it again!" The order came from Muzzafir. "I know it cannot be accomplished another time, slave!"

Matthew bowed, hiding his grin. It was the effect he'd hoped for, planned for. "Your wish is my command, O mighty master."

"I should think so, accursed infidel slave."

Matthew performed *The Mystery of the Disappearing Camel* a second time for Muzzafir. Then in answer to shouts from the drunken crowd he performed it again and again, nearly twenty more times. Rakik and Muzzafir's giddy men couldn't get enough. That was twenty camels, he noted to himself. Twenty fully loaded, fully fed and watered camels. A decent little caravan's worth. It was more than he could have hoped for. It was enough. Now was the time to move forward before suspicions were raised. Matthew turned from the false walls.

"Do you believe, great Sheik? Do you believe, mighty Muzzafir?" He didn't wait for their nods. "Then it is time to perform my next trick—magic so frightening that it will make your very toes curl!" Matthew strode back to the mound, leading all eyes and attention away from his dangerous hole. He reached for another, fresher torch. "I present to you now *The Coffin of Death!*

To the throb of drums, more of Asanti's men carried out the box Matthew had spent long nights working on. He'd planned to place it on the altar atop the mound, but as that was currently occupied by Cornwall, he settled for the area just beneath. He motioned the men to lower the box. They did so carefully, backing away from it with fear in their eyes. They'd been told who was to lie within it. Matthew approached the box and ran the flames from his torch over it, intoning bits of Latin nonsense. *"Ergo. Ipso Facto. Tabula rasa—"* Cornwall's favorite. He ended with *"Pro bono,"* and a heartfelt *"In Deo speramus,"* raised the lid, and spun back to confront his audience.

"I challenge you, Rakik. I challenge you, Muzzafir. Come and look into this coffin of mystery. Tell me if there is anything within that should not be within. Tell me if there are any secret compartments; any deviousness whatever about this simple box. I desire your true belief in my magic."

Rakik held up his hand, declining, but Muzzafir shifted himself from his pillows and rose in his mountainous majesty to ooze up to the "coffin." It was his ostrich-feather box, after all. He bent over and slowly stuck his fingers into each of the crescent-shaped holes, then, as Matthew held the torch over his head, peered suspiciously into its depths and tapped at all of its surfaces. Satisfied, he backed away.

"Is it as you remembered, mighty Muzzafir?" Matthew asked.

"Yes," Muzzafir allowed.

"Then I would ask a boon, O great master of slaves and men."

Muzzafir's suspicion returned. "Remember that you remain a slave, infidel. No matter your tricks. When we arrive in Tripoli, Rakik, who has been hoarding your services, will sell you at last into my keeping"—he smiled evilly—"and my pleasures."

"It is as you say, powerful Muzzafir." Matthew bowed with great deference. "Tonight I ask only the loan of your sword—and the swords of your men. Many swords. Enough to fill all these holes." Matthew had made dozens of holes. He needed dozens of swords. "Enough to skewer with pain and to inflict death upon the African woman who chooses to lie within . . . if the magic should fail."

Muzzafir's eyes lit with anticipation. The occasion was irresistible. He reached for his sword and offered it to Matthew. "I will grant this boon with pleasure."

Matthew bowed again as he grasped the handle. Then he watched Muzzafir snap his fingers. In a moment, the ground before them was littered with more swords than he could have dreamed of. Swords of pain and death. In his hands, swords of freedom. Matthew rose from his deep bow of thanks as Muzzafir returned to his pillows and snapped his fingers again. "The magic! I will have the magic begin now!" They were his swords, too.

Matthew confronted the assembled once more. "You will have the magic, honored guests. I call out for Afua, Queen of the Green Forests of the South, to fill this box, to partake of this magic!"

Asanti himself led his wife to the box. She had fixed her hair and greased her body. In the firelight she stood proudly for a moment, goddesslike—and slim enough from her desert march to avoid the sharp blades he must thrust around her, Matthew fervently hoped. Matthew took Afua's hand and helped her settle within the box. Asanti grasped one end of the lid, Matthew the other. Together they lowered it over the woman. She gave one frightened gasp; then there remained only silence. The two stepped away as the drums sounded again. Asanti took control of the torch, while Matthew had no choice but to grasp the first sword, Muzzafir's sword. He held it dramatically over his head.

"Afua, daughter of grace and life. Afua, wife of Asanti, mother of Asanti's son—I beg your forgiveness!" He plunged the sword through the first hole. A scream of fear erupted from the box. Or was it a scream of pain? Matthew felt sweat beginning to bead his face. Had he pierced her? He couldn't know. He must continue. He reached for the second sword. And the third. And the rest. Each plunge drew a gasp from the audience and a titter from Muzzafir. When there were no more holes to fill, Matthew stood back and wiped his face. He reached to Asanti for the torch. The African's eyes were rimmed white with terror, but he uttered not a sound. Instead, he evaporated into the shadows.

"Muzzafir!" Matthew roared. "Rakik! Is it your pleasure to inspect *The Coffin of Death* before the swords are removed?"

Once more Rakik refused, but Muzzafir returned with even more enthusiasm than before. His eyes glinted as he made a full circuit of the box, looking now like nothing so much as a vast, elongated porcupine. "This is a fine trick. A wonderful trick. I will remember it."

Matthew shuddered at the thought.

When Muzzafir returned to his place, the drums returned too.

"Asanti!" Matthew called. "Your wife awaits you!"

As the African reappeared, Matthew pulled the swords, one by one, from the box. The lid was raised. Matthew held the torch over the opening, afraid to look at what he had wrought. *Please, Robert-Houdin. Please let your trick have worked.* He finally forced his eyes open. Afua lay within, in a dead faint. Asanti gently wrapped his arms around his wife and lifted her out. Her eyes opened and she moaned.

Matthew stared. She was alive. There were drips of blood trickling from her arm and leg. He'd grazed her, but she was *alive*.

Asanti set his wife upon her legs and she stood, hanging on to him for strength.

"She lives!" the crowd exulted. "The woman lives!"

Matthew sank against the coffin as cheers rang

around him. Then he remembered the purpose of the entire exercise. *The swords.*

"Let the dance begin!" he bellowed.

Out of nowhere, masses of unchained Africans surged through the central aisle. Matthew remembered his next effect just in time. He bent to light the gunpowder surrounding the great dancing circle. The black people sprang over the fire like gazelles, carrying drums cobbled together from cooking cauldrons and food vats. The drums began again, until there was a wild frenzy of leaping, singing, writhing, and shouting within the circle. Matthew watched it build. Watched as Asanti and his special followers danced closer and closer to the forgotten swords. *Now*, he thought. *Now!*

Asanti read his mind. Suddenly there were swords raised in the hands of the slaves. Swords being turned on the unsuspecting masters. But there was something else, too. Something unplanned. A wild howl from the ramparts jerked Matthew's attention upward. His cheetah! His cheetah was outlined against the sky . . . leaping down from the walls of the fortress . . . leaping where? Matthew twisted to find Rakik behind him, the curved blade of his sword raised over his head.

"Your magic is nothing but deceit!" Rakik

growled. "You will pay for it with your life!"

Matthew had used up his supply of cleverness for the night. He froze in defeat, his eyes locked on the blade above him as the cat completed the arc of its leap. Onto Rakik's head. As the sheik fell beneath the claws with a shriek of horror, Matthew spun again. This time it was toward the high-pitched squeals of terror emanating from Muzzafir's throat. Matthew stared into the sky above Muzzafir. A huge, hewn rock was gracefully, inexorably tumbling from the crumbling tower toward the rigid slavemaster. As it collided with his skull, Matthew heard a cackle from on high.

"A present I send to accomplish right's end."

Offerings from the *jinn*! From Father Moses! Perhaps a little too enthusiastic an offering from Father Moses. A chip from his present glanced Matthew and he stumbled backward to clutch at his head as the Night of Nights completed its unfolding around him.

Chapter Fourteen

THE BLOODY CRESCENT MOON OF THE SAHARA squinted down at Matthew as he tidied up some of the night's loose ends. He turned from issuing another set of orders to find his great dog loping across the courtyard and into him. Down Matthew toppled. He gently pushed away the enthusiastic wet tongue to sit up on the hard-packed dirt.

"What brought on that hero's welcome? And where have you been all this time, Gin?"

"He was assisting me, *nasrani*." Above him, Hussein offered a hand and Matthew accepted it, struggling to his feet. "There was much to do outside the fortress walls. The caravan had to be assembled. Directions had to be given—"

The main purpose of the Night of Nights returned to Matthew. All its vivid drama returned, too. "Asanti and his people—when they slipped away, I had this mess to clean up. The bodies . . . the prisoners. Tell me how their escape went! What happened?"

Hussein grinned slyly. "In the madness of the final moments of your revels, I and a few waiting Africans managed to release another fifty riding camels, right through the main gates of Zuila! Asanti and his people are miles away by now, Allah be praised."

"But how will Asanti find his way?" Matthew asked.

Hussein straightened his wiry frame. "I, Hussein, desert navigator of some renown, set his course by the stars. Your chief need only follow these stars. He must travel by night and rest during the heat of the day. The caravan has water and provisions enough to reach the next oasis. After that Asanti and his people are in the hands of Allah."

Matthew rubbed his head. He'd had to ignore

the ache, but there was quite a large bump hiding under his turban from that fragment of Father Moses' rock. Right over the faculty for Hope. A vision of green, wet forests overcame him for a moment. "The Africans will succeed." He sighed, but not from despair.

"Asanti said one final thing, *nasrani*. It was a special message for you."

"What? Don't just stand there keeping me in suspense!"

Hussein's answer was laced with a certain pride. "Asanti bade me relate to you that his next two sons will be named in your honor: 'Matthew' and 'Morrissey.'"

It was Matthew's turn to grin. "That's a very fine message." As he peered into the night, other questions popped into his mind. "What became of the Tuareg and the Arabs who escaped our trap? I couldn't be everywhere, and I was busy dealing with the dead." He pointed to a dark pile nearby.

Hussein nodded. "We will bury them and the African martyrs as best we can in the morning." He gestured approvingly toward a white-robed, huddled mass at the far end of the courtyard. "It is satisfying to see how your revenge has become more Arabic in nature. How fitting for those slavers to be wearing Muzzafir's shackles."

Matthew smiled ironically. "A sense of humor sometimes helps. But the others? Those who escaped?"

"As for the rest, those not among your captured or fallen . . ." Hussein shrugged philosophically. "When Tuareg and Arab alike accosted me outside the fortress walls, I pointed out to their new leaders one thing."

Matthew bit. "What might that have been?"

"That which is completely evident, *nasrani*. With Rakik and Muzzafir dead, *they* were now in charge. And who was responsible for this unexpected elevation in status? . . . To receive mercy from those with much to gain is sometimes possible."

Matthew laughed, then stopped. "Where does that leave us? You and I and Dr. Cornwall?"

"There were negotiations, you must understand. It was a help that desert raiders are a superstitious lot. They appear to hold you, for one, in a certain awe."

Matthew squared his shoulders.

"I will not ask from whence you called up that giant cat, or the madman, either, but the hidden presence of these creatures—perhaps to strike out once more at your calling—will be a strong reason for the desert men to keep their promises."

Hussein's sharp eyes focused on a scuttling motion near his feet. *Splat.* He glanced up.

"Another piece of vermin no longer with us. . . .
And then there is Dr. Cornwall," he continued.
"Those he saved from the scorpions have chosen
to cast their lots with us." Hussein paused before
adding the decisive fact. "With them to help, and
a small caravan of our own original camels and
supplies, I believe we can safely make our way to
Siwa at last."

Hussein had been as busy as Matthew. The new
revelations were amazing, and it took Matthew a
long moment to register them all and ask his next
question. "When?"

"When Dr. Cornwall recovers from his struggle with malaria. That will give us all a few days to
rest and plan."

"Dr. Cornwall—" Matthew felt his body tense
for action again. "In the press of events I nearly
forgot about Dr. Cornwall! I must give him his
quinine. Where is he?"

"Where you left him, shivering with fever atop
your hill."

Matthew bent to rub Gin's head. "Come on,
boy. Let's go rescue the doctor from his sacrificial
mound."

When morning arrived, Matthew found himself
waking upon a proper mat within the walls of a

tent. It was the first time since he'd caught the
glint of burnished steel peeking over the rim of
that great dune ages ago. He relished the novel
comfort, then twisted in his blankets to find Asa
B. Cornwall lying next to him, eyes wide open.

"You're awake, sir! How do you feel?"

"As if I could wring out the fever sweat from
my clothing and irrigate the entire Sahara." He
propped himself weakly on an elbow while
Matthew reached for the next dose of quinine.
"Hussein claims malarial bouts go in cycles.
Two or three terrible days broken by a few
moments of clarity before it disappears to attack
as it wills, when it wills, throughout the rest of
your natural life. . . ."

Matthew administered the medicine with lots
of water while the moment of clarity remained.
After relating the night's events to the doctor and
making him as comfortable as he possibly could,
he emerged from the tent.

It was another clear, hot desert morning. What
would such heat do to the pile of bodies resting
through the night? Matthew set off in that direction, only to find the dead gone. Where? Surely
this rock-hard earth could not have been
broached that quickly. When he glanced toward
the far corner of the courtyard, he received his
answer. Hussein had risen even earlier and was

busily directing a crew of shackled Arabs. They seemed to be throwing objects down Matthew's magical hole. He trotted over.

Hussein nodded recognition. "The solution has been found, *nasrani*. The last of the bodies are even now descending into your tunnel. In a moment both ends will be sealed. The burial will be complete."

Matthew watched the final rigid form being lowered. "There were too many."

"It's no longer of import, *nasrani*. Here within the secret passageways of Zuila, Arab, Tuareg, and African alike will share eternity together. Perhaps they will grow in understanding."

Matthew continued to watch as the tunnel was closed and his mound was slowly shoveled back into its original home. Someday other travelers might venture upon the catacomb and wonder . . . He shook his head. So much death. He and the doctor and Hussein had to make it back to civilization. Asanti had to reach his green forests, or the effort would all have been in vain.

Hussein touched his shoulder. "Come, *nasrani*. This is finished, but there is still much to do."

By midmorning what remained of the Arab caravan was wending its way from the gates of Zuila, heading north to complete its journey to Tripoli. The Arabs would be poorer for the loss of the slaves, but still carried impressive loads of salt and ivory. Matthew and Hussein watched the departure from atop the ramparts of the fortress. Hussein was shaking his head.

"We could have had some of that salt and ivory, *nasrani*. It would have made us rich in Cairo."

"No," Matthew disagreed. "We want none of their ill-gotten gains."

Hussein sighed. "Speak for yourself, *nasrani*."

"Besides," Matthew added, "we want to give the Arabs no excuse to change their minds and pursue us to Siwa. Anyway—" He smiled and pulled something from beneath his robes. It was Muzzafir's iron key, the key to the shackles. He flourished it. "It will take a good long while for them to figure out how to remove those chains without this. A few days of such medicine and they may begin to rethink heading south for another *razzia*, another slave raid."

"You are still young," Hussein murmured. "You still believe the world can be changed."

"Yes." Matthew said it proudly. Then he stood quietly beside Hussein and watched as Rakik's old band of raiders, the blue men, slipped from Zuila to head west, farther into the Black Stone Desert.

The fortress of Zuila baked under the hot sun through the course of the long afternoon as the survivors slept. It baked silently, with only Matthew slipping between Cornwall's tent and across its courtyard to the castle to give assistance to the recovering patients. The silence became eerie, and Matthew began to imagine voices from Zuila's past rising around him. The voices seemed to be calling him as something—or someone—had before. He finally surrendered and returned to the ramparts where he had stood that first night. The night he'd had his third encounter with his *jinn*; the night he'd met Father Moses. He stared across the desolation of the Black Stone Desert, then began to concentrate.

He was in the exact spot. His cat had appeared from the tower—*there*. Matthew turned. Father Moses had materialized *there*. Matthew carefully paced the distance to the next tower, took a deep breath, fumbled with the match and candle he'd brought, shielded the fresh flame, and plunged inside. *Absolutely nothing mysterious about all this*, he tried to convince himself. *Nothing mystical*. Zuila just happened to be riddled with underground passageways and secret chambers. He descended.

The descent took even longer than he'd remembered. When he reached bottom, the coolness of the deep earth surrounded him. Also surrounding him was a maze of passageways. Which turn had Father Moses taken? He could get lost in here. So lost that his bones would be keeping company with those he'd watched being buried only this morning. Matthew heard Cornwall's voice. *Think logically, lad.*

He thought logically. Then he set down his candle and removed his robe. He picked at its hem till he'd pulled out a thread. He kept pulling. Soon his robe was shorter, and he held a ball of white cotton string. Matthew retrieved the candle and set off down the first corridor, leaving a trail of string behind him.

The first passageway led seemingly nowhere. Matthew retraced his steps and paused to leave a distinguishing soot mark at its entrance. He entered the second tunnel. When the smell of putrefying bodies enveloped him, he backed out in a hurry. The third tunnel led to the treasure room.

He stooped to duck under the low stone lintel of the gaping doorway and waited a moment, breathing the ancient air, feeling his heartbeat quicken. *More light.* He studiously avoided the center of the room and its contents while he made his way around the edges, lighting the half-gutted candles set into wall alcoves. At last he allowed himself to look at the horde. *It's only metal*, he told himself. *Shiny metal. Magnificently worked shiny metal.* Was it the gold that had been calling him back? Did he really care about the gold? He and the doctor had always managed . . . yet their war chest *was* depressingly low. . . . Would he be stealing if he took a few of these lovely things? From whom? Who even knew of their existence, except for—

"I see the gold glint in your eye."

Matthew wheeled away from the treasure. "You!"

Father Moses' humpbacked form had materialized out of the very air, from nowhere. But today he was leaning heavily on a stick. His wizened face—the most ancient face Matthew had ever beheld—cracked into a smile. One eye was clouded white, the other still sharp. "I told you true when first we met: the treasure is yours, for good to get."

"But it's too precious!" Matthew protested. "The tales it must tell—the history! It belongs in a museum like the Louvre!"

The old man shuffled a step forward and touched Matthew. When he spoke again, his voice changed. "Then this thing you must do. My days are numbered, this is true—" He coughed hard, then stopped and caught his wheezing breath.

His fingers had a palsied shake to them as he groped for something around his neck and with effort pulled it over his head. He beckoned Matthew closer. When he came, Father Moses formally—as if knighting him—slipped the golden chain over his head. Matthew touched the finely worked gold cross suspended from the chain.

"This belonged to Justinian of the Byzantine Empire," croaked the old man. "Now it is yours." A new fit of coughing overcame him and Father Moses stumbled aside to spit up blood. Matthew rushed to him.

"You should be resting, sir. Let me take you into the castle. Fix some broth for you—"

"No." Father Moses backed away. "Too long from humans I have been. I cannot face them—or their sin. . . . That rock I pushed sapped my strength, but the story—my story—must be told at length. . . . Take the treasure trove. Take as much as you can hold—" The old man collapsed.

"Father Moses! Sir! I need to thank you for what you've done. I want to hear *your* story! Don't go away. . . . There's been too much death already."

Matthew bent over the figure to pick up a skeletal wrist. He applied pressure to ancient veins, but could feel no pulse.

"Father Moses!"

Matthew collapsed to his knees among the useless golden treasures. It was too much. Too much drama. Too much death. Too much of everything. The weight of the past days nearly crushed him. He bent his head and cried.

CHAPTER FIFTEEN

Matthew hid his sorrows and his secrets until the doctor recovered from his malaria bout. At last, under cover of darkness, he led Cornwall up to the ramparts and to the second tower from the corner. Cornwall was still weak, and paused to catch his breath at the entrance.

"Are you sure you want to drag me down there, lad?" He peered skeptically into the inky chasm. "Are you certain it wasn't all a desert dream? Like your *jinn*? Perhaps a touch of malaria. I can personally vouch for the oddness of fever dreams. . . ."

"My *jinn* wasn't a dream, sir. And you yourself touched Justinian's coin—and my cross." Matthew felt for the heavy cross and chain hidden beneath his clothing, next to his skin, where he knew it would have to remain until they returned to Christian lands. The brief contact gave him courage to plunge into the blackness with only the pinprick of his candle, hauling Asa B. Cornwall behind.

Matthew's first concern after he'd illuminated the chamber was the body of Father Moses. Wanting to do the right thing, he'd laid out the old man with reverence along one wall, placing the gnarled hands across his chest, fingers carefully wrapped around a large golden cross from the hoard.

Cornwall gasped once at the glittering gold, shook his head disbelievingly, and followed Matthew to Father Moses. He knelt beside the body to knowingly feel the old man's skull, only to gently set the head down again.

"The tales this one could tell," he murmured. "Perhaps it wasn't a dream. None of it." He glanced up at Matthew. "Don't worry, lad. I haven't brought my calipers. I suspect the desert has mellowed me. One begins to learn the difference between fanaticism and grace."

He studied the leathery arms protruding from the old man's robes. "I think he was half mummified already when he died. In this chamber the process will complete itself. Who knows? We may be looking at the remains of the last of the desert hermits . . . an unsung saint." Cornwall stroked a hand, then creaked to his feet. "As for his treasure trove—"

"You see, it does exist! But what's to be done with it, sir?" Matthew asked. "Father Moses specifically gave it into my keeping. To do the best good, is what I think he was trying to say."

Cornwall rubbed at what remained of his jowls after the fever. "For starters, I believe it's best that our traveling companions know nothing of this, lad."

"Not even Hussein?"

"Not even Hussein. The average man would be overcome by gold lust. And really . . ." He reached for a small painting set within a jewel-encrusted gold frame, then dangled an earring from his other hand. "This sacred icon of Christ's mother; such jewelry—the only monetary value to be had in any of it would be by extracting the jewels, melting down the gold—"

"Melting down these treasures!" Matthew was outraged. "All the history would be gone! The art and craftsmanship. The stories—"

"Precisely. So we'll quietly pack up a reasonable amount—a selection of the best, as it were—and try to get it back to Paris, and the Louvre."

Matthew heaved a sigh of relief. "I hoped you'd see it that way, Doctor."

"Except for a few of the coins, of course," Cornwall continued. "There are more than enough of them to go around. More than enough to rebuild our war chest."

Matthew struggled within himself, and finally shrugged. Father Moses had willed everything to him, for some unknown reason. Maybe that reason was yet to be discovered and the coins would help.

"And Hussein will be given a decent share when we've safely arrived back in Cairo," Cornwall concluded.

Matthew smiled. "It's all right, then."

Within the silent embrace of Father Moses, the two began making their inventory.

On the fifth morning after the Night of Nights, the last caravan wended its way from the fortress of Zuila. This one headed east-northeast, out of the Black Stone Desert and back into the dunes of the great Sahara, cutting a straight line through the sands toward the oasis of Siwa.

Matthew exulted when the first dune grew large before them. He was astride his old friend Ali once more, with Gin contentedly padding by their side. "Look, Ali! Look, Gin! It feels like coming home!"

Ali delicately placed one foot, then the next, upon the shifting grains. He stretched his long neck and snorted with something akin to camel pleasure. Having paid his respects, he plodded on. Cradled within the old rhythm, Matthew beamed. They'd survived Zuila. They'd made it out of the Black Stone Desert. In a matter of only a week or two they'd arrive in Siwa at last. Never mind the new scars he and the doctor had added to their bodies and souls. Soon they'd be in Siwa. If the oasis answered at least some of the doctor's questions, from there maybe they could even think about going home. To their real home. That stopped Matthew's rambling thoughts for a long moment.

Where might their real home be? Paris? . . . New York? Matthew rubbed the grit of sand from his sun-bronzed face, considering. Did he and Asa B. Cornwall truly belong anywhere? Or had they become eternal wanderers? Matthew's mood darkened with the idea, and he rode on with it weighing upon his shoulders all the way to their night camp. But once in camp he wasn't given the opportunity to stew in his new gloom. Hussein was once more in full command, and glorying in it.

"Why do you sit and stare, *nasrani*? Get off that useless beast and help with the work. There are few enough of us now, and you have learned the ways." The guide stopped as Matthew made no show of moving from Ali. "Or would you prefer I carry a whip like the blue men?"

"No. Definitely not." Matthew slid from Ali with a rueful grin. Maybe Hussein was his family, good-naturedly bossing and nagging him the way his mother used to. Maybe the desert was his true home for now. Maybe he and the doctor would have to remake their home and family wherever they went. Maybe—as their old friend Voltaire used to say—that could be for the best in this best of all possible worlds.

Siwa Oasis was a burst of color and life almost unbelievable after months within the monotones of the desert. As it grew ever larger before them, Matthew's eyes widened. He'd pictured the oasis as being a few wells surrounded by drying palms. Or maybe something just a tad bigger—say, the size of Zuila. But Siwa Oasis spread out for miles. First there were scattered palms, next groves of olive trees. Small springs began popping up, and flocks of grazing sheep. Beyond the sheep a clump of camels ran faster than Matthew believed a camel could run. And in the distant, even greener core were hills dotted with holes, brown crumbling ruins, odd walls of stone. As they progressed ever nearer to the center, mud huts sprang up, people appeared . . .

Matthew gasped. *Women* appeared. Well, at least they were there. As for actually appearing—they were bundled up to the eyes and down to their toes more thoroughly than any veiled Tuareg. But they were women, moving with a grace that Matthew had almost forgotten existed—the grace Asanti's emaciated people had had starved out of them. Children appeared, too. They scampered from the huts to trail after the caravan, jabbering in a language Matthew had never heard.

"Hussein!" he called ahead. "What are these children speaking?"

"A Berber dialect, *nasrani*, known by few outside of this oasis. Siwa is very ancient, and has few visitors. You will hear some Arabic, but badly spoken."

"As badly spoken as my Arabic, Hussein?"

"It is impolite to seek compliments, *nasrani*," the guide shot back. "You know you speak like a native. Allah only knows how you came upon this gift."

Matthew grinned. It was one of the few compliments he'd ever received from Hussein, and worth waiting for. Wrapped in a cocoon of well-being, he rode Ali into the center of the town.

Hussein raised his arm for a halt outside a mud-walled caravanserai. Matthew and their odd complement of helpers had just begun the unloading chores when a slim figure darted from a nearby coffeehouse.

"Matthieu! You are alive! *Mon dieu*, Matthieu—"

That voice— He spun. "Nathalie? Here in Siwa?"

"Yes, yes, yes! Papa had business, so we took a boat, then came the short way from the sea, and—"

Words failed both of them, and they only stared at each other. Nathalie finally spoke again.

"You have changed, Matthieu. You are—how should I say—bigger. Older."

Matthew let out his breath. "And you are even lovelier, Nathalie."

They stared for another long minute. They both opened their mouths for the next words, but they were stillborn.

"Nathalie!"

She froze. "It is Papa, wishing me back under his wing. Why he even allowed me to accompany him on this journey, if I am to be forbidden to show myself, to even speak—"

"Nathalie!" The voice was more peremptory.

"I must go, but we will meet again."

Matthew caught her arm. "Where? When?"

She stared straight into his eyes. "At midnight. Where the oracle lives."

He relinquished her arm, but his hand was still tingling when Cornwall bustled up. "That exotic young lady. She looked the spitting image of Abdullah Abed's daughter—"

"She *is* Abed's daughter."

The doctor beamed. "Splendid. That means her estimable parent must be in the environs. What in the world could have brought him to Siwa in the heat of summer? Well," he rambled on, "nothing for it but to beard the man and find out." And Asa B. Cornwall set off for the doorway into which Nathalie had disappeared.

Matthew watched longingly, wanting nothing so much as to follow. Hussein, however, arrived first.

"The beasts deserve a well-earned rest, *nasrani*. I have arranged rooms for us within the caravanserai, and hired some of the Siwan boys to see to our animals. But first we must transport our belongings. We cannot leave them in the streets, the way we leave them outside on the desert sands."

Matthew roused himself from thoughts of midnight. Certainly a number of carefully selected panniers could not be left in the street. They couldn't be left in anyone else's keeping, either. He began unloading and transporting the golden hoard.

Matthew stood near the walls of the ruined temple under a gibbous moon. The light was eerie, and he could believe that fortunes had been told here, could almost hear the hollow, ancient voice of the oracle of the god Amun prophesying to Alexander. He shoved a hand beneath his robes to feel for the trinkets he'd placed in his pocket. Had it been wise of him to bring them? Would the gift be accepted? Would Nathalie even come?

Then out of the shadows her figure appeared. She'd thrown a cloth over her head, wrapped around her face in the fashion of the Siwan women. Matthew stepped forward.

"Nathalie?"

"Matthieu!"

She floated to him under the moonlight and raised a hand to his scar. "It is still there. That has not changed."

"No." He unwrapped her headdress. "And you have not changed in certain ways, either. I think you hold mystery within you. Do you live always in the shadows?"

She smiled as he touched her face in turn. "After you left Cairo, I was banished to my room for weeks. When I became wan, Maman begged my father to set me free. That is why I am here, but in a few more days—oh! To think our paths might not have crossed! In a few more days the great camel races my father came to attend will be finished, and we will be gone again, to Tripoli."

"So we have just a few days. And I'll be busy digging with Dr. Cornwall." Matthew decided to take the chance. He reached beneath his robes for his pocket. "I've brought you a present. They're very old, but in my heart I heard them cry out to live again—" He paused. He'd gone over the speech so many times in his mind. *Finish it.* "On you, they will live."

The moon shone on the Byzantine earrings in his hand. Its rays made the gold and dangling jewels almost throb.

Nathalie hesitated. "Emeralds?" She reached out and set an earring in one lobe, then the other. She tossed her head. In that instant Matthew felt drawn back thirteen hundred years to Constantinople. He could see Nathalie gliding through the gilded court of Justinian, her head high and proud. Belonging.

She smiled acceptance. "But I have no gift for you . . . except—" The young woman leaned forward and offered her lips to Matthew. His heart stopped beating for a precious moment. Then she spun and fluttered off into the shadows once more.

"Nathalie!" But she was well and truly gone.

Idiot! he chastised himself. He'd let her disappear again. And he'd learned little more about her, or if he'd see her again. All he'd really learned was that he was smitten. Hopelessly. He turned to stare at the ruins behind him.

"Prophesy, O Oracle. Tell me what's to become of this affair!"

Matthew could have sworn he heard an answering chuckle. But maybe it was only the scuttling of lizards across ancient stone. He sighed, and slowly made his way through deserted streets back to the caravanserai.

CHAPTER SIXTEEN

In the half light just before dawn, Matthew noticed something he'd missed in his first exuberance over arriving in Siwa. He'd missed the skulls. Donkey skulls. After spotting the first one, he discovered they were everywhere about the town: hiding in the byways of crooked alleys; mounted over gates; leering down from mud walls. Donkey skulls impaled on long sticks. He shivered and turned to Hussein, trailing behind him.

"These skulls . . ."

Hussein rubbed blearily at his unshaven jaw. "Against the evil eye. Siwans take no chances."

Perhaps it was only the chill of the early hour, but another tremor passed through Matthew. Skulls might be his business, but not this kind, used in this way. He avoided the next one and increased his pace to catch up with Dr. Cornwall.

Asa B. Cornwall wasn't taking any chances either. He'd finally made it to Siwa, and he was going to do his job right. Shortly after dawn he and Matthew and a crew of Siwan men under Hussein's direction were already working at the Temple of the Oracle of Amun. Cornwall stood back to oversee the beginnings of progress with a proprietary air.

"This is not at all like skulking around cemeteries in the old days, eh, lad? Here we've got the headman's permission, and plenty of men eager to work for their wages. Amazing what a little *baksheesh* will do." He rubbed his hands with enthusiasm. "We're going to excavate until we find something, Matthew. I can feel it in my bones. Someone's here."

"But the missing mausoleum in Alexandria—" Matthew tried.

"Tosh. Alexander's remains were moved so

many times, everyone finally lost track of them. And what better place for him to end than where he began?" Cornwall beamed as the first load of dirt was carried past them in a great basket on the head of a laborer. "Yes, indeed. Beginnings and endings. I truly believe Siwa is going to answer all of our questions."

"I hope so, sir. I truly do." Matthew left the doctor to his dreams and went off to inspect the acropolis in the light of day.

All work stopped for lunch and rest during the worst heat of the afternoon. Cornwall was propped against a mighty stone column in the shade of what remained of the temple roof. He was gently snoring. Matthew brushed a few flies from his face and braved the sun to continue his explorations. He climbed to a pinnacle above the ruins to get his bearings. Behind him was the dozing town, while past the temple mound in the plains below were groves of date palms that ranged as far as a line of distant parched hills. The mountains rising beyond were the limit of the horizon, the limit of the oasis. The sun was so fierce that the sky above everything was bleached white, rather than blue. Matthew squinted through the glare, searching for he knew not what. Not far off, his eye caught a glint. Water? One of the many springs of the oasis?

What he discovered was a deep pool of bubbling water nestled within the palms.

"Eureka!" he crowed, scaring away a few perching birds. In moments he'd flung off his clothing and was blissfully submerged in the pool. This is what he'd dreamed of all those long days journeying across the sands. *Water.* And here it was. Not exactly enough to launch a ship in; not even enough for a good swim—but enough. He plunged under its coolness again, then regretfully pulled himself out to return to the temple. By the time he arrived, he was hot and dry again, his momentary euphoria dissolved in the heat. It didn't help that when he found Cornwall in the same spot—still snoring—he found something else as well.

"No!"

His exclamation woke the doctor. "What is it, Matthew?"

"There. Right above your head!"

Something had been added in Matthew's absence. It was another of those impaled skulls.

"Well, well," Cornwall commented. "The word does get around. Someone has discovered we're searching for skulls. A kind thought, but not the correct mammal, I fear."

"But sir, this has nothing to do with Alexander—"

"Be kind enough to rouse the workers, lad. Time is marching on, and we've much to accomplish."

Three days passed excavating the depths of the oracle's temple. Three days passed without another sight of Nathalie. The only discoveries were new donkey skulls mounted around the dig each morning. The Siwans might be hungry for their wages, but they still weren't comfortable with unearthing the dead. Matthew became increasingly uneasy. His experience with *jinn* had taught him that not all superstitions were foundless. *Something* unpleasant was in the offing. Cornwall, however, was oblivious to everything but his quarry.

"Did I ever mention Plutarch's comments in his life of Alexander, Matthew?" He didn't wait for a response, just chattered on over the sharp thuds and clinks of dozens of men wielding shovels and picks against dirt and stone. "Alexander could be munificent. He gave away a hundred fortunes to his soldiers. Then again, he also speared his best friend Clitus through the heart in a drunken rage."

"Who needs a friend like that?" Matthew

asked. Try as he might to equal the doctor's enthusiasm, his patience was wearing thin on the subject of Alexander the Great.

"An ignoble thought, lad. Majesty always has its little quirks." Cornwall gazed off across the distant plains as if summoning up visions of his hero. "Alexander would footrace only with kings, yet he said that if he were not the lord of the known world, he'd choose to be like the penniless Greek philosopher Diogenes. You remember, he's the one who wandered around the streets looking for an honest man."

"And lived in a tub," Matthew added. "I really can't see Alexander the Great living in a tub."

"Perhaps not, but never forget he was a man burning with ambition, grappling with his demons like the rest of us—"

"*Effendi!*"

The shout ended Cornwall's musings.

"*Effendi!* Something has been found!"

The doctor gasped, then sped toward the excitement. Matthew trotted after him.

The laborers had opened a gaping hole on one side of the temple sanctuary. Cornwall himself had chosen the spot in which to begin because of the curious markings worn nearly smooth on the stone pavers of the floor. Now the paving stones were cast aside, and one of the Siwans was eight feet down, bending over a dark pile of encrusted rubble beginning to emerge from the earth.

"Out of the pit!" Cornwall commanded. "The discovery could be fragile. I'll deal with it myself." Hussein translated the order, and in a moment the doctor was deep in the hole himself, yelling to Matthew. "Hand me one of those brushes! A soft one. And a spade!"

Matthew sent down the tools, then hunkered over the edge to watch the progress. Around him, curious Siwans did the same. Cornwall fastidiously chipped and brushed, chipped and brushed, till at last the shape of the objects before him emerged.

"It's a cache, Matthew!" he shouted. "A cache of weapons and body armor. The kind that would have surrounded the burial of a great warrior!"

Matthew felt the sharp intake of his breath. His earlier indifference disappeared with his excitement. He tried hard to keep that excitement within bounds. "Are you sure, sir? Could it really be Alexander at last?"

"Who else would be buried here besides the oracle? And the oracle would be surrounded by graven images, not weapons. Still—" Cornwall wiped sweaty hands on his robes, leaving damp brown streaks on the cotton. "It's going to take hours to ease out these finds without doing damage to them. Come nightfall we should have the answer."

Matthew leaned closer. "I hope so, Doctor."

Hussein and the laborers had long since grown bored with watching Asa B. Cornwall's tedious work. They'd decamped for their suppers, and the sun was rapidly setting over the oasis before Cornwall was sitting in rapture over the bits and pieces that he'd finally allowed Matthew to cart from his pit.

"Look at this, Matthew!" he exclaimed for the hundredth time. "A piece of a scabbard! Of the correct period! And a sword, hilt and all!"

Matthew, too, had grown a little dubious with the passing of the hours. "But they're all green and nasty, sir. Nothing like Father Moses' treasure."

"Bronze. That's what happens to ancient bronze. Almost like rust." He rubbed at the sword's hilt and scabs fell away. "You see! There's a design underneath, a raised design." He rubbed some more. "Good heavens! It appears to be . . ." Cornwall peered more closely. "*A ram's horn!* Matthew! That was the sign of Zeus-Amun, the symbol Alexander took as his own after meeting the oracle! This very sword could have belonged to Alexander the Great! And this—" He picked up a larger bit. "Almost half of a shield. This, too, might have been held in his very hands!"

Matthew's stomach rumbled. He was anxious to return to town for the evening meal, true. But he'd also had in mind prowling around the walled compound where he now knew Nathalie was staying with her father's entourage. Somehow the pull of the very alive young lady was becoming stronger than that of a long-dead world conqueror. "Aren't you the least bit hungry, sir?"

"Food? Who can think of food at such a time! Find me some lamps or torches. We're proceeding without the workmen. Even if it takes all night." And with that, Asa B. Cornwall threw himself back into the artifacts pit and began scrabbling in the dirt.

"Sir? Doctor?"

It was no use. Matthew had long since learned that a phrenologist in the heat of discovery couldn't be reasoned with. He headed for the equipment pile to fetch a lantern. He'd barely gotten it lit when the sun seemed to blink, then completely slid below the horizon.

"Light!" Cornwall yelled. "Where's my light?"

"On its way, sir."

Grumbling to himself about the endless day, his empty stomach, and his frustration over

Nathalie, Matthew delivered the lantern. Cornwall snatched for it and hauled it into the pit. Bent again over his task, the doctor and the light both disappeared. Matthew sighed. He really ought to bring another lantern. No sense in the doctor working half blind.

En route to fetch it, he passed the small pile of ancient objects Cornwall had been gloating over. Matthew bent for the sword—Alexander's sword?—and raised it above his head. It was cumbrous and heavy, not at all like the balanced swords of modern Arabs. And its fighting surface certainly couldn't compete with curved blades of burnished steel.

Matthew slashed the weapon through the air, then brought the tip closer to flick off more effects of the ages. He fingered the results. Amazingly, the blade's edge was still sharp enough to prick him. Matthew set the sword down to rub a little sand over the cut, the way the Tuareg did. That's when he heard the sound.

Leaping to his feet, Matthew spun in its direction. Camels were coming from the town. They were only dim shapes in the deepening twilight, but he made out two of them. Who could it be?

"Company coming, Doctor."

"Eh?" Cornwall's head popped out from behind a column. "What?"

"Camels headed this way."

"Make them go away. I don't want to see anyone. Don't want anyone messing with my discovery, either." He popped back out of sight. "Tell them I'm not here . . . absolutely no disturbances . . ." His mumble faded away.

Matthew obediently stood guard before the steps of the temple, waiting for the unwanted visitors.

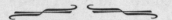

Almost as suddenly as the sun had set, the moon rose. Tonight it was full, and its bright light fell squarely on the procession of two.

"Mr. Abed!" Matthew gulped. It was Nathalie's father, looking none too pleased. And behind him on the second camel was Nathalie.

Abed prodded his camel to its knees with the hilt of his whip and decorously dismounted. He'd traded his usual fez and Western clothing for the turban and robes of the desert. He wore them well, looking every inch the powerful man beneath them. He advanced on Matthew, his whip brushing him aside like an insect.

"Where is your master?"

"Dr. Cornwall?

Abed deigned to stop and turn back toward Matthew. "Of course, Dr. Cornwall. Where is he, boy?"

It had been a long time since anyone had called him *boy*. Dr. Cornwall's endearing *lad* he'd never minded. Yet Abed's *boy* raised his hackles alarmingly.

"He's not here."

"Then why are you?"

Matthew stiffened his spine. "I'm guarding the site."

Abed stared up and down Matthew's form, the whip in his hand trembling with some unknown fury. "Then it's you I'll deal with directly. I'll tend to the doctor later." He turned. "Nathalie! Dismount and approach!"

Matthew watched Nathalie do her father's bidding. As she crossed the courtyard before the temple, the rising wind blew her loosely wrapped head scarf to her shoulders. Dark hair swept down her back, and the earrings—his earrings—glinted in the moonlight. As she tentatively paused, Matthew involuntarily felt his chest tighten anew at her loveliness. He had to remind himself to breathe.

"Come forward, daughter!"

Nathalie moved again, a puppet under her father's control. Abed grabbed her arm. He pointed at an earring. It jangled evocatively to its own music. "This discovery I made tonight." He ripped the earring off and thrust it in Matthew's face. "*Where* did this come from? Are *you* responsible for this demeaning of my only daughter?"

"Demeaning?" Matthew stepped back in shock. "How could a gift, such a gift—ancient jewels from the Byzantine court of Constantinople—" He had to swallow back his hurt and rising anger. "How could such a gift demean your daughter?"

Abdullah Abed's whip lashed out, just missing Matthew's face, but striking his shoulder. Hard. He refused to flinch.

"She is not yet of an age to receive gifts. And when she is, *I* will be the judge of who is worthy of giving them. You have dishonored my only child! You have impugned her honor!"

"Papa—" Nathalie finally spoke up. "Papa, I told you it was completely innocent—"

"How could such jewels, such gold, be innocent?" raged Abed. "Your reputation has been besmirched, *ruined*, by this infidel nobody! I won't be satisfied until I learn of their source."

"But, sir—" Matthew glanced toward the temple where Cornwall was hidden, oblivious to the turn of events. No point in seeking help from those quarters. He tried again. "The treasure of the Emperor Justinian is untainted, like your daughter. I would never—"

Abed's eyes flicked. "Aha! You admit the treasure! You admit there's more!" He discarded his daughter, to raise the whip again. "Tell me, slave. Where it came from. Where you've hidden it. Confess, or you'll regret it. Every bone in your body will regret it."

Now Matthew was really angry. He glossed right over the threat of bodily harm. "*Slave?* I'm no one's slave! Not even Sheik Ibn er-Rakik could keep me enslaved. I'm a free man, an American citizen—" Matthew stopped. The word had come entirely too easily to Abed's lips.

The whip slashed down again. "If I say you are a slave, it becomes so. Have not my ancestors, have not *I*, enslaved half the continent of Africa already?"

"*You!*" The experiences he'd survived in the desert rushed back to him. Answers to questions born with Asanti and his people were at hand. Matthew moved forward, on the offensive at last. "You're on your way to Tripoli, to the slave markets—"

Abed barked out a laugh. "It's unnecessary to dirty my hands at any slave market. The profits are brought to me. I need only issue a few orders, keep an eye on my employees. Make certain that their greed does not exceed its bounds. My web of power stretches everywhere."

Matthew stood eye to eye with the man. "You're more evil than Muzzafir."

Abdullah Abed smiled. "One of my best lieutenants."

"Not anymore," Matthew boldly informed him.

"What do you mean?" This time Abed took a step back. Then he dug in. "You evade my question. What of the treasure?"

"So it's not your daughter's honor that really concerns you, is it?" Matthew brazenly asked. "You're using Nathalie—"

The whip slashed out once more. "*Never* speak my daughter's name again! What of Cornwall? You are protecting him. He is never far from you. Produce him at once! Cornwall will tell me the truth of this matter. Cornwall could *never* lie to me."

He surely couldn't, Matthew thought. Not once Abed had tested his tortures on the doctor. His ear caught the soft clink of spade against something hard. He needed to distract Abed before he heard Cornwall's labors too. He needed to protect his friend.

Enough confrontation. Now it was time to consider defense, as well as a diversion. Matthew edged away from whip distance to trip over something. Without missing a beat, he grabbed it and sped toward the camels.

"Stop!" Abed cried. "How dare you—"

Matthew slid onto the saddle of the first camel, begging it to rise.

"Good fellow. Up now."

He stroked its neck, continuing his endearments, using the voice Ali loved. The camel responded. By the time Abed had pursued him to the second animal, Matthew was already urging his camel past the ruins of the oracle, down onto the plains spread out below, clutching to his chest the sword of Alexander the Great.

Abdullah Abed followed, abandoning Nathalie to the moonlight and the ghost of the oracle of Amun.

Matthew risked a quick glance over his shoulder. His heart dropped. Abed was almost upon him. And he'd had such a start on the villain. How could that be? . . . Nathalie's passing remark from his first night in Siwa returned to him, and finally made sense. Abed came to Siwa for the races. . . . He trained racing camels. . . . The man must be riding one of them now. That meant there was a chance he was, too. Matthew gave his beast a sharp prod. As if by magic, it broke out of its careful plodding gait to lope, then gallop, across the landscape.

Matthew laughed into the wind. The silhouette of the town was to his left, its minarets rising toward the stars. The ridge of mountains was to his right. And he was racing through the plains between them, going he knew not where. But he was going *fast*. He had a chance. Asa B. Cornwall had a chance.

His elation was short-lived. Abed's camel began gaining on him. Matthew kicked his mount in a new direction, off toward the nearest hill. As it grew larger in the moonlight, he saw strange holes tunneled into its slope. It was the necropolis of Jabal Almawta, the mountain of the dead. Hussein had spoken of the place. If he could make the distance, Matthew knew he could hide in one of the tombs. There were thousands carved into the stone. Abed could search days for him.

With the tombs looming ever closer came thoughts of his *jinn*. If ever there was a moment when his personal *ifrit* would be welcome, it was now . . . too late. Too late for the thought. Too late for the wish. The clatter of pursuing hooves grew louder. Abed was overtaking him.

Matthew turned to see Abdullah Abed speed ever closer. Twenty yards . . . ten. At five yards his whip flicked out. Matthew watched, mesmerized, as it curled past the face of the moon, undulating like a snake. Waited for its cutting lash. . . . But Abed hadn't angled for Matthew. Instead, he'd cleverly aimed the length of braided leather for the neck of Matthew's mount. The camel gasped, groaned, and came to a choking halt. Matthew stared at the necropolis almost before him in despair. The unwinking black holes gaped back at him. The dead would not be helping him tonight.

Too soon, Matthew felt the sharp edge of steel against his throat. Abed's dagger.

"Dismount, *slave*," he ordered. "*No one* turns his back to Abdullah Abed. *No one* steals his prize camel. *No one* refuses answers to his questions. Your chance at life flew with your escape attempt. After you've revealed all, you'll have the pleasure of bleeding your last drops of blood under the desert moon."

Matthew moved to obey, and the dagger's pressure let up. Alexander's sword was still in his lap, unseen, nearly forgotten. It set off a strange heat, and it almost seemed to be humming. No, it was a different sound that came to his ears: the deep purr of a great cat working up to a mighty growl. The growl came forth, ringing through the night. It became a cry emanating not only from the sword, but also from the necropolis before him, and the desert surrounding him.

His *jinn* lived.

Casting despair to the winds, Matthew exulted in the strength-giving roar, the fortifying vibrations. He firmly grasped the sword of Alexander the Great and in one fluid movement swung the blade through the sky in a circle that encompassed Abdullah Abed—

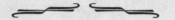

Nathalie was waiting when Matthew led the two camels back from the plains onto the temple mount.

"Papa, have you come to your senses? And you too, Matthieu?" She ran up to the animals. *"Papa!"* Her long shriek filled the night.

Abed was slumped over the second camel, motionless. Matthew urged his own animal to its knees. Wearily he stumbled back to the solid earth. "Nathalie . . . your father . . ."

"Papa! Speak to me!" Nathalie frantically prodded her father's lifeless body. Then she turned on Matthew.

"How could you? I trusted you, Matthieu!"

"Nathalie," Matthew tried again. "He gave me no choice, Nathalie—"

Unhearing, she flailed out in fury with fists and nails. "He's dead. You killed him. *Pig of an infidel!* You murdered my father!" Tears streamed down her cheeks as she furiously slashed at Matthew's face. "*Honorable* man. This is the return you give my father's hospitality! This is your thanks! I'll give you another scar that you'll never forget. I'll gouge out your eyes—"

Matthew caught her raging hands at last. "He cared nothing for you, Nathalie. It was the treasure he was after. He tried to murder me. For the treasure. He had his dagger to my throat—"

"*Pig! Lying pig!*"

Matthew grasped her more tightly. "He treated you like a prisoner, Nathalie—"

She pulled away to rip off the last earring and throw it to the dirt. She stamped and ground the gold and jewels into the earth. That done, she spat in Matthew's face for good measure.

"You know *nothing* of my father, Matthieu. His greatness was beyond your understanding. I'll prove my usefulness to him! I shall continue his work."

Her fury vented for the moment, Nathalie turned and defiantly marched to the first camel. Shortly she was upon its saddle, urging it to rise, leading her father's body back to town.

Matthew slowly wiped spittle and blood from his face. Then just as abruptly as Nathalie, he spun and headed for Asa B. Cornwall's hiding place.

"Dr. Cornwall, sir, I think it might be best if—"

"Matthew! Where have you been? You missed the momentous moment! The crowning achievement of my career and life! After Napoleon, of course." In the flickering light of the lantern, Cornwall proudly displayed a dirt-encrusted skull. *"Alexander the Great,"* he intoned.

"Perfect timing, sir." Matthew grabbed for the skull, then the doctor. "Let's just get Alexander wrapped up and be on our way. I strongly suspect we're about to overstay our visit to the oasis of Siwa."

CHAPTER SEVENTEEN

MATTHEW STOOD ON A SHIP ONCE MORE—THIS TIME at its stern. He wasn't juggling. He was gazing back at the port of Alexandria as it slowly dissolved into sky and water. Asa B. Cornwall leaned against the deck rail beside him, Gin standing guard over the old satchel by his feet.

"It would seem that we made good on our escape from Abed's minions, lad."

"Yes, sir," Matthew muttered.

"Why so glum? We're returning to Paris with

Alexander the Great! Not to mention a full war chest—even after making Hussein the richest guide in Egypt!"

"Yes, sir." Matthew sighed.

"And the Louvre—the Louvre will be the beneficiary of the best collection of Byzantine objects outside of Istanbul. Why, the French might even be pleased enough to award me one of their medals. I'd look well with one of those ribbon things around my neck, wouldn't I, lad?"

"Yes, sir," Matthew mumbled.

"Snap out of it, Matthew! That girl was her father's daughter. Trouble through and through. And besides, you're much too young for affairs of the heart anyway."

"Just because *you* never—"

"Enough." Cornwall fumbled in a coat pocket. "Here. I was admiring Justinian's trove last night, and this turned up in one of those little jewel boxes." He held his fist out to Matthew.

Matthew listlessly accepted the object. Then he looked at it. "Bigger than a coin . . . gold." He turned the medallion over. And gasped.

It was his *jinn*. His cat. Etched in full life: bared teeth, extended claws, springing at a hidden prey. "But—"

"I think you'd best take good care of that, lad. Sort of a talisman, eh? We might need his help when we take off for our next expedition."

Matthew smiled at last. "And where might that be, sir? *Who* might that be?"

Cornwall's eyes twinkled. "I've about had enough of the desert myself. I had in mind something on the order of, perhaps, Justinian?" The doctor patted wisps of hair across his bald pate as the sea wind rose. "Then again, there's farther east to consider as well. Tamerlane? Genghis Khan?"

Matthew grinned. "There's still a lot of world out there."

"And heads," Cornwall added. "Never forget the heads, young man."

Fig. 2.

Craniometer.

THEORIES OF IDEATION

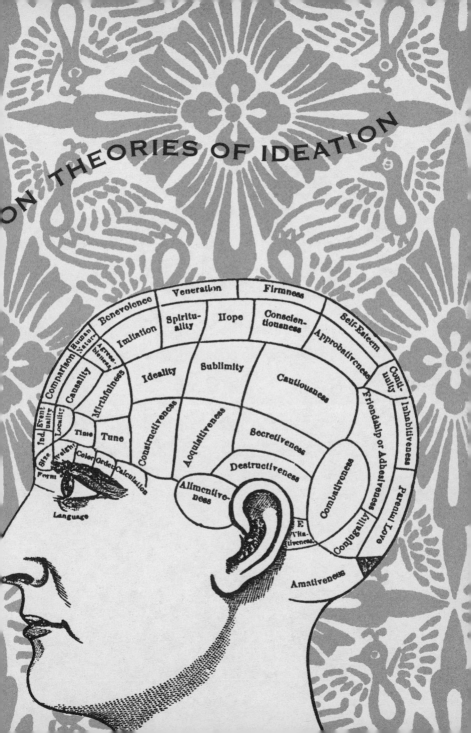

ON THEORIES OF IDEATION